First published 2020.

Thinksheet Publishing

www.chrisjoneswrites.co.uk

Books by Christopher P Jones

NOVELS

Berlin Tales Trilogy:
Berlin Vertigo
Vanished in Berlin
Berlin Vengeance

ART HISTORY

How to Read Paintings
Great Paintings Explained

Christopher P Jones writes historical, mystery and literary fiction. He is fascinated by the possibility of opening up a window into the past and imagining what it was like to be there. He is also an art critic and art historian.

Berlin Vertigo is his first novel. The second instalment of the Berlin Tales series, *Vanished in Berlin,* is out now.

To find out more, go to www.chrisjoneswrites.co.uk

BERLIN VERTIGO

By
Christopher P Jones

Berlin Vertigo

THE ASCENT

"Man lives only once in the world" – Goethe

1

Potsdam, Germany. 1928

Inside a bar, a man in a tuxedo climbed onto a glittering stage and struck a brass gong. All the faces steadily turned towards the sound, as cigarettes were stubbed out and conversations hushed and ended. The man disappeared into the shadows; and in his place a woman emerged, stepping out from the darkness and into the spotlight. She wore a full length satin dress, a long pearl necklace, black gloves up to her elbows, and painted eyebrows that ticked upwards like apostrophes. A piano player hidden in the wings began to tinkle a series of high-notes that gradually built into a pulsing rhythm. With this, the woman began to sing.

The music spiralled through the room and wound around the circular tables like a serpent. As the audience relaxed into the performance, toes tapped and more cocktails were ordered. Couples flirted with each other. And in this place, where the walls were painted absinthe-green and cobwebbed chandeliers hung from the ceiling, anything was possible.

At the back of the bar, two friends stood watching. They had spent the evening drinking in the taverns of Potsdam town, some twenty miles from Berlin. Now, satiated with drink, they smoked and settled into the

3

entertainment that Clärchens Bar offered every weekend to its paying guests.

Thomas and Erich were old friends. They had been friends for at least fifteen years. They came from opposite corners of Berlin; Thomas from the final shabby stretch of the Kurfürstendamm, Erich from the high-end suburbs that skirted the edges of the Tiergarten park. But none of these differences got in the way of their friendship. They could talk endlessly about the latest gramophone records, the latest books they'd read, their favourite women, the cinema or nightclub that had recently opened in Berlin, and just about anything else in between. Over glasses of beer, they ate from a plate of cold-cut wurst and sweet rye bread, and let the music enliven them in happy spirits.

At around midnight, the two friends were approached by a young man. He had just entered the bar; as he spoke, his teeth flashed white between the strands of an overgrown beard.

'I'm sorry to bother you,' the man said. 'I hope you don't mind me asking, but do I know you?'

Thomas and Erich looked at each other.

'I don't think so,' Thomas replied. He smiled at the young man, who appeared nervous, as a way to calm him. Thomas always trusted his smile. He thought he could win anyone over with a gracious grin.

'I thought I recognised you.'

'Not us,' Erich replied more curtly.

'From the factory?' the stranger persisted. 'Orenstein and Koppel. They make railway engines, carriages and freight cars. I used to work there. It's only a few miles from here.'

'I think you've mistaken me for someone else,' Erich said.

'Please. I'm just looking for a familiar face.' He

turned to Thomas. 'Are you sure you don't know Orenstein and Koppel?'

Thomas shook his head.

'In that case, I'm sorry, I must have made a mistake. I saw you both from a distance and thought I knew you. I'm so embarrassed.'

'That's fine,' Thomas said.

Now he began to see that the man was much younger than at first glance. Looking closely, he was no more than a boy. He wore a pair of wire-rimmed spectacles that, along with the beard, disguised the face of a teenager.

'I never thought I'd be in this position,' the young man went on, raising his voice above the music. 'I'm due to be married. I'm a father. Now I've lost my job.' He gave a self-pitying chuckle. 'There is no work to speak of. I've been staying at the hostel upstairs from here but it costs more than I can afford. I just need to find someone who can help me. I thought you might be from the factory.'

Thomas began to dig around in his pocket for a few coins. 'I'm sorry, but we're nothing to do with Orenstein and Koppel. Here, take this.'

Thomas held out his palm.

'It's not enough,' the boy replied flatly, turning Thomas' hand away.

'Ungrateful swine,' Erich responded. 'You ungrateful wretch,' he said louder.

'I just don't know where to turn,' the boy pleaded.

'Why don't you pull yourself together?' Erich went on. 'What's the matter with you? Where's your wife? Where's your child? You're here begging money from us, then when you're offered it, you refuse.'

Thomas put his arm across his friend. 'Stop it Erich,' he said.

But Erich didn't stop. 'I detest this kind of thing. Our country is sick with people like this. Beggars and animals.' He began to push forward. 'When are we going to see vermin like this cleaned up? We're too soft on men like this.'

'I'm sorry,' the lad said. He turned to Thomas. 'I'm truly sorry.'

'Take the money,' Thomas said, deciding it would be the last time he offered it.

'Put your money away,' Erich said. 'He'll only waste it. That's what men like him do. They squander their lives. It's happening all across Berlin. It's a sickness. You try to help them and they throw it away. He's destined for the same thing as the rest of them. Dope-addiction, then prison. Mark my words.'

'Maybe you've had too much to drink,' Thomas suggested in a vague attempt to excuse his friend. As he spoke, the boy glanced up at a clock on the wall and began to move away, disappearing through the bar door before Thomas had finished his sentence.

'There you are,' Erich said. 'He's not interested. He's gone. Ungrateful lowlife pauper. We'd be better off without rats like him.'

It was the brink of morning by the time they found their way home. Only clouds obscured the first blue hints of sky that might have illuminated the doorway to the apartment block. Exhausted, the old friends fell into silence as they climbed the stone staircase.

On entering the apartment, they bid each other goodnight. The hallway was dark and both men trod carefully, trying to remember the location of ornaments and other objects to avoid – like naughty children who had stayed out too late.

Just then, a strange sound came from the door they

had just come through. It was a sort of scratching, followed by a distinct click. Erich put his finger to his lips and Thomas fell quiet. Together they watched as the door began to open. Through the bluish shadow, the figure of a man emerged, as quiet and cautious as a whisper.

His frame was small and hunched as he crept in. He moved through the cavernous dark like a key through a keyhole. Advancing further, he was unaware of the two men standing only a few feet away. The figure drew past them towards the living quarters, and once in the adjacent room could be heard sifting through drawers and cupboards.

Erich tiptoed over to Thomas. 'A thief,' he said excitedly. Then, not hesitating for a response, he followed into the living room with just as much carefulness as the intruder. Thomas paused, rolling up his sleeves in case he needed to pounce or else defend himself. Whoever this intruder might be, the combination of drink and adrenaline shored up his courage.

At the doorway, he heard Erich call out. A panicked cry followed – the thief had been interrupted. A moment later, two bodies flew past Thomas' nose, the second in pursuit of the first. A crashing of doors and floorboards. Suddenly the action had moved out to the roof terrace that adjoined the apartment.

Thomas followed. Outside, the dawn light was threaded with an uncertain orange, shifting imperceptibly like the hour hand of a clock. The thief dashed out onto the patio. Erich was close behind. The light grew and the breeze moved across, and on his face Thomas felt the cold air as he came to the door. He could see the thief charging about in mad circles, looking for an escape route. Thomas was summoned to guard the door.

The power of Erich's tall frame loomed over the thief, whose increasingly slight shadow swung like a pendulum from one end of the terrace to the other. There was a chair nearby; the intruder took it and began swinging it in wide arcs, banging it against the terrace floor and clanging it against the railings. But this hardly detained Erich's charge, which was fast and flying, so that in a second, the chair was cast to one side and the thief was seized with two large hands.

The boy struggled as Erich asserted his weight. When held still, Thomas could see his face. Undoubtedly it was the same face as the boy in the tavern. The beard was the same ragged brush, and the glasses, thin wire-framed with circular lenses, were just the same too.

'It's you,' Thomas said.

'He must have followed us,' Erich said.

'I don't believe it.'

The young man didn't say anything, but just wriggled inside Erich's grip. He seemed so small and malnourished that it was clear there was no hope of him overcoming it.

Still, Thomas thought, it was best to find something to tie him with. He went to the kitchen and rummaged through a drawer, where he found a length of rope and some strips of material cast-offs. The rope was strong, but the material might be more appropriate, so he brought both. Now back on the terrace, he felt suddenly relaxed, as if he was quite right to think about binding the boy until the police could be alerted, and moreover was fulfilling his duty with practical efficiency.

Yet as he headed back out onto the terrace, instead of hearing the familiar groans of the boy tussling under Erich's grasp, a sharper cry now accented the air. No longer the whimpering moans, but a scream of undeniable fear.

Thomas chased out to the terrace. There he saw Erich with the boy in a new sort of embrace, more aggressive on Erich's part.

'He swung at me,' Erich shouted out as he shoved the intruder against the iron balustrade.

The thief-boy struggled some more. Erich took hold of his lapels and shook him like a rattle, then in one strenuous manoeuvre, pulled him away from the iron railings and raised him clear off the ground. In the same motion, he bared all his weight and lifted him upwards, pushing him over the edge of the railings into the abyss on the other side. The boy yelled in horror as he toppled backwards. Over he fell, quickly and immediately, into the miserable gash of blue darkness.

Thomas watched on in astonishment. They were eight floors above street level. The thief's body succumbed swiftly to the shadows of the brickwork corner, disappearing into the dark heart. He screamed as he fell. Seconds later, there was a heart-sinking thud.

It was hard to fathom. The intruder had been cast onto the other side of the balustrade, the wrong side, the imponderable side.

Thomas raced forward to the edge. It was all dark below, the young man's fate indeterminate. For a moment there was silence, then the whir of a motorcar echoed along the avenue beneath them, causing his heart to jump. Then the clocks of Potsdam chimed six o'clock. He turned to Erich, who came up close, full of life, hot and twitching, his hair fallen forward. 'Quickly!' he said beneath his panting breath. He clutched Thomas' arm as he moved past. 'Quickly. Let's go.'

9

2

One day earlier

A blue steam locomotive arrived at Potsdam station from Berlin. Inside the fourth carriage from the front, a group of friends stood rocking with the rhythm of the train, peering out of the windows for Potsdam city to come into view. They might have taken the steamboat service that ran through the lakes, a journey that made for a sedate afternoon in the summer months, but the train was altogether faster and more exciting. Besides which, there was work to be done.

As the train slowed along the final stretch, a station guard, who had been made aware of the day-trippers' arrival, followed the carriage along the platform on foot. He swung open the carriage door and with a gloved hand gestured for the group to come forward.

The reason for their special attention focused on the unique cargo they were transporting: a seven-foot-long artist's canvas draped in a white sheet. Thomas was at the front of the object; two of the other travellers held onto the rear corners, and alongside them, the artist, acting as the chaperone and foreman.

The station guard led the group through the platform, waving his hand to part the crowds ahead of him. Thomas watched on as this petty-official escorted the canvas through the dispersing crowds of passengers. The way the guard led with great theatrical gestures, stepping over luggage and dogs-on-leashes beneath his feet, all the time fluttering his white gloved hand ahead of him, made Thomas laugh.

For now, the canvas was unmarked. It was a huge piece of material stretched taut over a wooden frame, an empty space, a decision not yet taken. The artist, a young woman by the name of Jana Constein, treated it with detached indifference save for the practicalities of moving it between locations, as if its value was yet to be determined. However for Thomas, it was already an object of fascination, an intriguing promise of things to come.

He'd heard that Jana Constein was one of the rising stars of the Berlin art scene, a portrait painter who had studied under the much-admired Herr Wolfsfeld at the Berlin Academy. She later became his star pupil, and for her final two years of study was given a studio of her own as a prize. As a painter, she kept to enough rules of perspective and realism to win the admiration of traditional art-lovers, whilst with her nudes and portraits of 'new' women, she also broke enough rules of social decorum to appeal to the avant-garde too.

Out on the street, Potsdam seemed as attractive as ever. Thomas smiled, thinking with sweet regret how infrequently he had cause to visit the old city. As he looked around the open space doused in sunlight, he saw hats and feathers, fur stoles and walking canes, and all the other expensive garments suggestive of a well-heeled town. It was the city of palaces and fountains, with the Sanssouci Park and its Greek allegory frozen in stone, headlands of Rococo architecture and banks of Italianate staircases lined with corals and shells rising from the park floor.

He remembered the events of that morning back in Berlin, how he had washed in a hurry, dressed eagerly and ran down to the street with no reason to question how it was he had fallen into this unusual arrangement. A man such as him, having his portrait painted! By a highly esteemed painter! He'd recently met the artist, this Fräulein Constein, and it was said by certain circles that she had great prospects. It was a real opportunity that had come up, the kind that seemed to emerge once in a blue moon! That he'd been selected to become part of a work of art was a compliment.

Around the station at Potsdam the scene was vital and energetic. People moved in a hurry. A bearded organ-grinder rolled up, wheeling his music-making contraption onto the middle of the street. He began turning the machine's handle so that a wheezing melody filled the air. A few moments later, a young girl, who was wrapped in a dark coat and an Arabian shawl, began dancing to the melody and singing in a shrill voice that hardly matched the eerie syncopations of the organ.

The friends lifted the canvas onto a horse-and-cart and placed rolled-up tarpaulin bundles beneath it to stop it from sliding. The driver of the vehicle, who wore a cape and had white slicked-back hair like a peeled onion, climbed onto the cart and occupied himself with the job of unknotting the tangled reins.

Thomas walked at the front of the procession alongside his friend Erich. As always, Erich seemed to take the lead in the day's proceedings.

'Are you ready for this?' Erich asked.

'For the painting?' Thomas replied.

'No, I mean for the girl. You'll meet her today. Do try to impress her.'

'You mean Käthe? Oh, I almost forgot about her.'

Erich grinned. 'I'm sure the two of you will get along

12

famously.'

Thomas was not altogether comfortable about being set up with a stranger. 'I don't know,' he said with a frown. 'We haven't set eyes on each other yet.'

'Just try your best. Only, when you are both deeply in love, don't forget who brought you together.'

Erich winked and woke up a smile on Thomas' face.

As always, Erich wore expensively tailored clothes, the colours carefully chosen to match the gush of dark auburn hair that fell back in waves from his forehead. As they walked, taking the city street by street, with church bells constantly clanging and horses hooves clopping in front of them, the two friends remarked that it was a bit like walking ahead of a funeral cart.

Their destination was an apartment with a large roof terrace that overlooked the city. On arrival, Thomas noticed there was a stone plaque on the wall beside the main entrance engraved with the word *Ruppin* – he guessed that the building had been named after the old medieval town in north Brandenburg.

After carrying the canvas up eight flights of stairs, the group explored the rooftop in admiration and relief. Thomas led the chorus: 'It's perfect,' he said, stepping up to the iron balustrade and forthwith feeling he had the right to say something grandiose. 'What a painting this will turn out to be!'

The terrace was set high above the rooftops of the old town, stationed between the bell-towers of several handsome churches whose beating chimes met the terrace like waves lapping against the hull of a ship. Its floor was tiled in terracotta and around the edges there were clay flowerpots with geraniums and petunias in bloom.

Thomas introduced to Käthe, for it was her apartment they had overrun for the afternoon. She had a pretty face and long dark hair with a ribbon tied through it. She was helping the artist arrange things: a long table with a white tablecloth spread over it, with fruit and pieces of broken-up bread across the top, and a knife and some half-filled glasses of beer.

Then it was time for the rest of the models to position themselves around the table's edge. They were to do so in the manner of luncheon guests who had just finished a meal. To begin with, the artist instructed everyone to approach the table in a spontaneous spirit, to find a place to stand or sit of their own choosing. Then, for the next ten minutes, she went between each model and made adjustments to their posture: a wrist here, a shoulder there, the upturn of an eyebrow, the downturn of a gaze. When everyone was ready, she insisted that all must remember their poses for future sittings.

Presently, the bells of the city struck midday. Thomas glanced across the sea of buildings that made up Potsdam, painted in the northern palette, of shades of tawny-brown and khaki, soft-purple and terracotta, and for a moment felt touched with contentment. These were the colours the artist would use in her painting – he understood that.

He decided then and there that he loved that rooftop and all the other rooftops out there. He let his eyes move steadily along the jagged horizon pierced with church spires. Here was a view he could really enjoy, honest as the air floating above them.

As his gaze moved, he tried to catch Käthe's eye, to pass on his contentment. But she was locked in admiration of the city too, submerging herself in the same view as he was.

'Thomas! Hold still please!' Jana called out from beside her canvas. Promptly he returned to the posture

14

he had drifted from. 'Everybody? I'm sketching you first,' she said, 'so you must hold perfectly still!'

And hold still they did, inert like shop mannequins. There seemed to be something valuable in the endeavour, something ineffably pure in the act of staying motionless on this cool spring afternoon.

Until at once a fierce gust of wind came thrusting across the terrace, throwing everything into disarray: tablecloth and canvas, and the models' positions interrupted. It seemed to come from nowhere.

From Käthe, the wind plucked the ribbon tied around her hair. It fluttered on the breeze, weaving through the air like a bat at dusk. Immediately, Thomas leapt to his feet and reached over the side of the railings, catching the garment with the tips of his fingers before it could snake away into the deep chasm below. He handed the ribbon back, as Käthe smiled back at him.

Erich leaned over and whispered into Thomas' ear, 'Well done. Every girl loves a hero.'

It was from that moment on, with the unsettling wind and Erich's sly comment, that something changed that day. Looking back, it was so subtle, so unbecoming of that happy moment, that there could have been no way of foretelling the dark events that would unfold following that sanguine afternoon.

3

As the evening wedded with night, Thomas and Erich went drinking in the bars of Potsdam town. After the gathering on the roof terrace earlier, they accepted Käthe's offer of a bed for the night and decided to remain in Potsdam until morning. Tonight they would cement their friendship afresh and celebrate the artistic events of the day just passed.

They went to a bar with a cabaret show where the singer sang in both German and in French. Between each song, the pianist rose to his feet and handed her a single red carnation.

After a while, Thomas noticed a group of three soldiers sat in the corner, eating roasted ham hock and drinking from thick glasses of beer. They were *Freikorps*, war veterans who had joined one of the many private armies that had sprung up across Germany in the past few years.

Thomas eyed them suspiciously. They didn't seem suited for the bar. They wore long coats and had rifles by their sides – weapons left over from the last war. He wondered what they were doing here and if they intended to cause trouble.

Erich glanced over once or twice. He seemed far less concerned about their presence. 'That reminds me,' he said as he stubbed out a cigarette. 'I have a story for you.'

Thomas pushed his drink to one side and focused his attention on his friend. The bar they were in receded into the background.

'It's about a soldier,' Erich started. 'Hard-working, honest, the sort of man you would be glad to be friends with. Can you imagine him, spruced up in his uniform and heading off to war with a keen heart? It seemed like a good thing, a heroic thing, to take his place in the trenches with his fellow brothers-in-arms.

'Life on the battlefield was hard, of course. The stench of death lay like a fog over the miles of wasteland, growing heavier and thicker by the day. But our man was resolute. He held his nerve, undaunted. He fought the good fight. That is until one day, when he saw a rainbow above the land and it reminded him there was still beauty in the world. From that moment on, as if from nowhere, he was afraid of dying. It came on suddenly and intensely. He couldn't fight it. It felt like a ghoul was clinging to his back. He could no longer stand the idea of fighting a war and dying for his country. His response was to run away. He fled his regiment and hid among the low-lands, in the bogs and canals, too afraid to go home. He stayed out of sight for nearly three years, living like a wild animal, stealing food and sleeping in woods. His family were told he was missing in battle. His mother and sister took to their mourning clothes and slowly accepted their loss.

'Three years later, the soldier finally decided it was safe to go home. By now, his appearance was so wretched that it was hardly surprising he wasn't recognised by his mother and sister. When they saw the silhouette of a man coming towards them, they took a great wooden mallet and struck the intruder down with a single blow. Killed him outright. It was only when they lit their lamps and looked into his eyes that they recognised him as their own kin. What made it worse was they had only just surfaced from three years of grieving from the news of his death. Now they would have to grieve all over again, only this time with themselves to blame.'

Erich adjusted the parting in his hair, marking the end of the story. He paused for a moment, waiting for Thomas to respond. He went to take another cigarette, but changed his mind.

'It's just like a Greek tragedy,' Thomas offered.

'Why so?'

'Families turn on themselves, everyone is in a state of confusion. That's how war affects things.'

Erich nodded. He gave a half-smile. He seemed oddly agitated, as if Thomas had given the incorrect answer.

'Fate is out of our hands,' Thomas said, trying again. 'That's the lesson, is it not?'

'Yes, sort of,' Erich said with more than a hint of disapproval. He seemed to want Thomas to catch hold of something more, to see a meaning that he wasn't prepared to say out right.

Erich was like that. Full of tales and declarations that he expected others to learn from. It was like he was trying to guide Thomas to a more enlightened view of the world. When Erich acted like this, Thomas could never quite rid himself of the feeling that Erich was a better positioned man. He was wealthier, more secure in his life, and he possessed an inner confidence that made him fearless.

What's more, he had his beautiful fiancé, Ingrid. And he had his family, that old Berlin family with roots in the ground as deep as an oak tree and as wealthy as a family could be in these times. Erich had been groomed to take up a commission in Germany's burgeoning colonies and would have done so had the war not intervened. Erich's father continued to support his son with a monthly allowance, tolerating the extravagances that Erich was well-known for.

Thomas and Erich were completely different. Thomas didn't quite earn his living in a factory, but it wasn't that different. At the print rooms of the *Berliner Tageblatt* newspaper he worked as a typesetter, arranging letter-blocks on the presses ready for the midnight copy run. The work was quick and unforgiving. It was a noisy place, with its printing machines, spinning pistons and cranking arm-shafts. He had been in his post for many years, by which time he had become one of the more adept compositors there.

Whereas Erich – well, what did Erich actually do? He did all the things that the son of a grand family did: he stepped in and out of 'positions', he advised on boards, consulted, lent his support, sponsored others. The last time he was known to have had an actual job was working at the Reichstag as part of the legislature. Any more details, he was never in the mood to reveal.

Thomas would like to feel some of those privileges himself. He would like to have arrived, to move with Erich's tailwind and perhaps one day catch up with him. That was his hope in any case.

It was at that moment that a young man approached them in the bar. He had a beard and wire-rimmed spectacles.

'I'm sorry to bother you,' he said. 'I hope you don't mind me asking, but do I know you?'

4

After the fall

The two men hurried out of the apartment. What would they find? All at once Thomas felt sickened to his stomach. He was convinced that an inanimate heap of twisted bone and flesh awaited them at the foot of the building.

He remembered Käthe was also at the apartment – had she slept right through it? He thought of her as they left. Had she not heard the fracas on the terrace, with all its banging and yelling? He wondered if she might in fact be awake in her bedroom, listening with fear and confusion, her ear pressed to the door.

As the two men dashed down the spiral stairwell to the street, he thought about turning back, until he noticed Erich's lapel. There were fingernail marks scored into the leather. He pulled Erich to one side and pointed to the scratches.

'Look at these.'

'He must have lost his grip,' Erich replied.

Out on the street, where the dawn light was rising fast, morning traffic had begun to swell and the life of the town was stirring. The corner of the street buttressed a sheer stone wall. From this dead-end, only a single exit was apparent, yet nobody passed the two men as they approached.

The drop must have been eighty-feet and the cobbles underfoot were as hard as ice. The chances of surviving such a fall seemed impossible. Yet as they rounded the corner, they realised that no hint of the boy remained, not even a spot of blood, though a plethora of filth on the ground would disguise more or less anything.

'Where has he gone?' Thomas asked. The men paced further around the edge of the grubby red bricks. High above them they could see the faint suggestion of the black railings of the roof terrace. Thomas scampered back on himself, peering up to the terrace. A fall from there would surely kill a man, wouldn't it? And yet, as the minutes passed, no sign of the boy materialised.

'Erich! Where is he?' Thomas asked. He glanced around. The walls about them were tall, narrow and dark.

'Come here,' Erich called.

'Have you found something?'

'No, but we shouldn't stay here,' said Erich beginning to walk away.

'But what about the boy? How do we know he's alive?'

'Why do we care?' Erich's face was flushed and agitated.

'Because we… Because we have to find him.'

'Someone must have taken him away. That's obvious isn't it? He must have called for help.'

'Have they? But who?'

'It doesn't matter. Come on.' Erich urged Thomas by the arm as a convoy of horse-carts passed behind, clopping and crunching the top-gravel.

'But he's disappeared.'

'So let's go.' Erich came up beside him and grabbed his elbow. 'Thomas,' he said, 'I'm not waiting around. We have to leave before someone sees us.'

21

Erich strode off and disappeared around the corner.

'We simply can't leave like this,' Thomas called out as he followed. He was aware of the town waking up around him, aware of the possibility of being seen. But he didn't care. He grabbed Erich's jacket and saw it was ripped beneath the armpit. The jacket was made of finely woven wool with broad leather lapels, tailored long, just as the young rich men of Berlin liked their jackets.

'Look at your jacket.'

'What about it?'

'You'll have to explain that rip. People will ask you.'

'You need to keep your voice down.'

Thomas took a step back. A tide of confusion was rising inside him.

'Listen Thomas, there's nothing here.' Erich's tone began to relax. 'There's no trace at all. It's as if nothing ever happened. That means there's nothing for us to worry about. Don't you see?'

'Let's just look around some more. Maybe we've missed something.'

'We haven't missed anything. He must have fallen on something soft and escaped. Perhaps there was – I don't know. All we can say is that it was his lucky day. He slipped and fell. Then he got lucky.'

'He slipped?'

'He lost his grip.'

'You pushed him over!'

'I did not!'

'I saw you lift him up and push him over. I saw you with my own eyes. I saw you Erich.'

'Yes, well, make of it what you will. Come on, let's go.'

'What's that supposed to mean?'

'What?'

'Make of it what you will?'

22

'Exactly as I say. Listen, whatever happened to that boy, in my opinion, he deserved it.' Erich stared back directly at Thomas. His blue eyes began to sparkle.

'I don't understand you,' Thomas replied.

'The way I see it, you should be pleased we found nothing.'

'Pleased? No, I'm not pleased. For all we know, that boy was dragged off as soon as he hit the ground. He broke every bone in his body and died in the arms of someone trying to save him.'

'It's possible,' Erich said. 'But don't let your mind run away with itself. My advice is to forget it ever happened. It's over with.'

Erich paced off towards the main street. By the time Thomas had caught up, Erich's thoughts had begun to wander.

'Do you think an event like this can change your life?' he turned and asked, his voice suddenly bright and inquisitive. 'I would never have thought it could, but now I'm having second thoughts. We did something extraordinary today. And extraordinary things change lives. You would expect it. Wouldn't you? I demand it!' Erich held out his arm theatrically. 'I demand it change my life!'

'And how would it change you?' Thomas replied. 'Do you want to get locked up for murder?'

'Sometimes we have to accept the consequences.'

'You may have killed someone this morning – are you ready for the consequences of that?'

Erich laughed. 'That boy! It was the least he deserved. I told you, he's part of a sickness.'

'He deserved to die?'

'Listen Thomas, I hope the boy is alive. Of course I do. I'm simply talking about the experience. The pure experience of it. Of never knowing for sure. Don't you understand that?'

'Yes, I understand it because there's no trace of him. Who knows what his fate has been?'

Erich patted Thomas on the back. 'This will seem like a great joke to us in a few years. Probably in just a few hours. Mark my words.' Then he came closer. 'We are two great human beings, you and I. There's no need to let this event divide us. Now, I'm hungry. I'm going to find something to eat.'

The sun was gaining in height now, and as the light lifted, marks on the paved street began to reveal themselves and for a moment became bloodstains, until the light shifted again and the stains reverted back to the commonplace grime of a street alley. Thomas couldn't help but dwell in the same spot, his thoughts locked in shock and disbelief. Every mark on the ground was evidence, but he had no idea how to account for it.

Then, after a few minutes, he noticed a man coming towards him, a man in a uniform: it was a local police officer. He was smoking a cigarette and was looking out across the street with a mindless air. He walked slowly, with a sleepy expression on his face and passed Thomas without a glance.

Now a whole set of new thoughts entered Thomas' mind. Could he tell the policeman what had happened? Should he tell him about the boy and what Erich had done to him? Without further deliberation, he dashed after the officer. In that moment, he was convinced he was going to tell him everything about the events on the terrace, to relinquish every detail he could remember. Erich would have to pay for his actions. That was the moral law and he was in no position to contravene it.

All of a sudden, Thomas felt he had right on his side, as if the great tide of fate had lifted him to this moment in time. Maybe it had always been lifting him, even if he wasn't aware of it until now. It had delivered upon him a duty, to put aside the provincial landscape of friendship and think about his place in wider humanity. It was clear what he had to do next.

5

Thomas approached the policeman and placed himself directly in his path. The officer didn't seem at all phased by the interruption. His eyes were focused on a distant plane, perhaps watching a flock of birds rise and fall from a line of rooftops. He stopped and began to smile, then calmly invited Thomas to unburden his troubles.

But Thomas froze. He could not talk. One man looked at the other; the second man looked expectantly at the first. In the spur of the moment Thomas felt divided and awkward. Betraying his friend was impossible. He hesitated, and in that hesitation, his resolve crumbled.

He suddenly felt self-conscious. He didn't want Erich to see him talking to the policeman. He gave a resigned, frustrated smile. The policeman, not wishing to waste any more time, turned around and continued his serene patrol in the opposite direction without a word.

Thomas made his way up the staircase. A minute later Erich appeared behind him.

'I saw you with that policeman? What on earth has got into you?'

For the first time, and with some relief, Thomas recognised a hint of fear in his friend.

'Nothing. I didn't say anything to him.'

The two men carried on upwards, sharing between

them a deepening silence. In the apartment they found Käthe putting on her coat before a full-length mirror.

'My god, have you boys been out all night? I'm about to go to work and you two are just getting in!'

'Did we wake you?' Erich asked with imponderable lightness.

'No. I slept like a baby. It must have been all the events of the day.' She smiled at Thomas. He caught sight of himself in the mirror and found his face to be drawn and pale.

'Night time is when all the most interesting things happen,' remarked Erich as he strode through towards the terrace.

Thomas followed, feeling ashamed to the core. 'We'll be going home soon,' he said.

'There's no need to rush off. You must stay as long as you want. Rest if you need to.'

'Thank you. That's very kind.'

Out on the terrace, Erich leaned against the railings and didn't say a word. He was more placid than ever. Thomas paced back and forth. He was tired and wide awake at the same time, alert to the possibility of finding some clue to the whereabouts of the boy. All at once it seemed like a vital task and a terrible dream.

'I'm thinking of taking a trip to Rügen Island,' Erich said, gazing out over the rooftops. 'You can come with me if you like?

'Rügen Island? Off the coast?'

'It is very beautiful there. Chalk cliffs and sandy beaches. We could have a holiday.'

'You're thinking of a holiday at a time like this?'

'We can sunbathe and swim all day long. It would be in a few months' time, when summer comes. I'll bring Ingrid and you can ask Käthe if you want. A holiday might be just the thing for all of us.'

'I'm not going to Rügen Island.'

'Have you been before?'

'No.'

'Then you should consider it. It's really very beautiful. And don't worry about money, I'll pay for it. Promise me you'll think about it.'

Thomas couldn't listen. All this talk of Rügen Island was absurd. He began to loathe his friend. It was a crisp, brittle feeling, the only feeling he could really hold onto.

The morning passed. For some reason, neither of them wanted to leave the apartment, as if a strange magnetism was keeping them together. Thomas sought out a secluded corner of the living room and pretended to sleep, whilst Erich moved around coolly, eating whatever food he could find and flicking through books from Käthe's shelves.

Later, Thomas took himself outside onto the terrace. It was hard to believe that only a day earlier he had stood there and declared how beautiful the view was. It didn't seem so attractive now. It seemed like a murderous height. Waves of shock began to churn through him. A boy has been killed! He wanted to shout it down from the balustrade and draw people to the bottom of the building, to hear him and acknowledge what at this moment couldn't be fathomed.

Instead, he went and stood beside the railings. He stayed there, baffled and yet mindful. There was something truly odd about what had taken place, something alien in the way Erich had turned to violence so quickly. Things didn't add up.

Thomas looked down to the street far below. Everything looked so small. It felt as if he could reach down and pluck a lamppost or a tree from the earth with a simple pinch of his fingers. Then he noticed something. A metal fire escape on the face of the adjacent building, zig-zagging down the brickwork. He thought it might be worth getting to, as it could offer a new vantage point.

He stepped away from the railings and went through the apartment, not saying anything to Erich. He descended to the floor below, and from there, through two doorways before finding his way into a corridor that led to the fire escape. He descended down the twisting heights of the metal staircase until he stood only two floors up from street level. From here the town was not so distant. He could see things more clearly, and being alone now, he had time to think.

It started to rain. As the rain grew heavier, he began to see something on the ground below. Where the rain was making the cobblestones wet, shapes were beginning to emerge. He waited and watched. At the very spot where the boy would have fallen, to his astonishment, he could see something appearing. With the rainfall, an outline began to darken. Finally, he could see a series of contours on the ground. It was an angled form, with a hooked limb and a bent arm.

Within the next minute, ripening on the street-floor below, he saw the silhouette of a body. My god, he thought. The body itself was not there, but with the falling rain its stamp was unmistakable. Two arms and two legs twisted around a torso. The body had fallen and smeared on the ground. Here was the residue. There could be no doubting the trace left by the boy.

He returned to the apartment fixated by the image he had seen. In his absence, Käthe had returned.

'Oh Thomas, Erich was just telling me about last night,' she said expectantly.

'What exactly has he told you?' Thomas replied, alarmed.

Just at that moment, Erich stumbled out onto the

29

terrace, all brisk and smirking, a drink sloshing in his hand. As he went, he tripped on the step and fell forwards, stretching out his arm to stop himself.

'Damn it! Look what I've done,' he called out. 'Did you see that? I tore my jacket.'

He held up his arm and there was the torn armpit, all open and sagging with loose threads.

At this, Thomas realised Erich hadn't said anything about the thief boy. Instead he looked on in shame. This is how it will be, he thought. This is how the story will be crafted by Erich into a series of accidents and mishaps, and finally made to disappear.

'What have you done?' Käthe asked.

'My mother bought me this jacket,' Erich replied brightly. 'She will be so upset. Let's drink to that!'

Käthe broke into laughter, passing a happy glance to Thomas. 'You're terrible,' she said to Erich. A grin flashed across Erich's face as he disappeared back into the apartment. A short time later, he returned with two further drinks. 'I made up these rum cocktails, I hope you don't mind,' he said, handing one drink to Thomas and the other to Käthe.

Thomas took it without a word and drank it in a single gulp.

'What's the matter with you?' Erich asked jovially.

'It's time we left.'

'Nonsense!' Erich's voice grew bullish.

'Thank you for your hospitality,' Thomas said turning to Käthe, 'but Erich and I are leaving now.'

'Okay, Thomas you win,' Erich said. 'Us comrades must stick together.' Then turning to Käthe, he remarked, 'Thomas and I will always be brothers in arms.' Erich gripped his friend by the shoulder and led him towards the door. Thomas could feel Erich's hot alcoholic breath rolling over him.

He knew then that a pact had been made, even without his consent. He knew it all too well. And as the two men made the heavy trek back to the train station, keeping close to the street walls and ducking their heads from the light of passing motorcars, he knew it was Erich he had given into, Erich who had taken the upper-hand, just as he always did.

6

The next morning, Thomas woke up in the familiar domain of his Berlin apartment. It was a long and narrow room, made up of a series of alcoves divided by curtains that provided space for a kitchen, a dining room and a bedroom. In those quarters, he'd become an expert in frugal living, not only in monetary terms but in spatial economy too. The only way to make the room physically habitable was to do away with furniture. When, occasionally, a visitor came around, they would always make the same comment – 'How could you possibly live like this?' – which annoyed and pleased Thomas in equal measure. (He remembered someone once saying, 'Your room is so inhospitable it's offensive,' much to his amusement.)

His building sat incongruently at the end of a row of lavish residences opposite a theatre. The building was a slim, three-storey tenement house with eleven rooms. It was a crumbling, downbeat structure that clung to the end of a well-mannered cast of apartments like a parasite. Here was the story of Berlin in a single architectural anomaly.

He went to the window, drew back the curtain and mindfully sifted through the people on the street below. He looked along to the end of the Kurfürstendamm. If he pressed his face to the glass and looked to the left he could just about see the Gedächtniskirche, that strange and lonely church residing among a mêlée of car horns and newspaper sellers.

In the beginning, the building had been an exciting place to live. All manner of people passed through – lawyers, actors, chefs, students, soldiers, artists – some on their way up, many on their way down. At times, it felt like a series of life-lessons passing before his eyes: the variety of ways a person could be thrown into success or cast into failure by circumstances beyond their control.

The long-standing proprietor of the whole apartment block was known as Herr Beenken. Now here was a man of pitiful appearance! By the age of fifty, he had the look of a man twenty years older. His face was marred by a string of uncommon illnesses that stole from him any hint of vitality. He smoked a pipe all day and through most of the night too, out of pure boredom mainly, never pausing to step out into the wider city, which was too daunting by far. Rumour had it that Beenken once had a son who ended up on murder charges. They said he set light to a motorcar with another man inside it in a botched attempt to fake his own death. The rumour also said that he went to the guillotine for it – not that Beenken had ever hinted at any of this to Thomas. Most of the time, he was a lonesome presence inside the building, to be found sat beside a window somewhere, firing his pipe and sending swells of blue smoke upwards from his overweight silhouette.

What made matters worse was that Beenken had taken a distinct liking to Thomas as if he considered him a true friend. His visits to Thomas' room were as predictable as they were punishing. They consisted of the usual creak of the bannister, the slow whine of the floorboard by the door, and that revolting cough – a sharp hak, hak, hak. Then the turning of the key in the lock – an intrusion Thomas had no power to stop. Through the gap the old man's face slowly slid into view, grinning apologetically as he shuffled in with new linen, his little eyes creased up behind little spectacles, the trace of pipe-stink and fetor carried in on his clothes.

'Did you hear?' Beenken said that morning as he arrived into Thomas' room, 'about the latest resident driven out for falling into arrears? All his clothes thrown out into the street? He's a destitute now.' Beenken had recently hired some hard-nuts to take care of the rough and tumble, and spoke now in fascinated tones as if referring to some remote piece of hearsay, not his own handiwork.

Beenken wore the same musty tweed suit every day. The jacket was too large, and the trousers, lacking a belt or pair of braces, were worn halfway up his torso and required pulling up every half-minute or so. He paused by the chair, ran his meaty hand across his brow, pushing his side-parting back into place, then cast his eyes around the room, hoping to start a conversation that might prolong his visit. His face trembled and his round, rubicund features were a picture of illness. His eyes were puffy and pink, and between his lips a small array of two or three grey teeth poked through and seemed to be there regardless of whether his mouth was open or closed.

Presently, he raised his finger in the air to make a point and began muttering the beginnings of sentences only for them to slip into nothingness as his train of thought derailed. He continued to do this for the next three minutes, pottering about the room as he did, and was just about to leave when finally he hit upon something solid to delay his exit.

'Yes, yes' he said, as if halfway through a discussion.

'I have been lucky to land on my feet. These few rooms bring me a comfortable income, and given my age, this life of leisure is fitting. I suppose that's the way of things.' He paused until another thought came to him. 'Have I told you? I have taken to reading philosophy in my spare time, and believe I am an excellent pupil. I am reading the great Schopenhauer, whom I am sure you have studied yourself?'

Thomas shook his head.

'He is a most interesting character. One day we shall have to discuss his Distinctions. But – ah yes, that can wait for another day. Suffice to say, I receive enough income from these few rooms to see me through to my expiration. It is a sufficient income, and I have you to thank for that.' Beenken smiled his very best paternal smile. 'And what is more, I won't have to sell my war medals now I have this convenient pension – they were my nest egg you know? And they are highly prized. You are aware that I have many admirers in the museums of Berlin who would do just about anything to get their hands on my medals? Oh, they would pay a lot for my collection from the last war, and especially for my Frederick collection, which I keep in a very special hiding place. Yes, yes. It is true, Frederick was a diplomat of the first order. I know you have a grasp of history so I won't talk too much about Silesia, but let us agree he was also a military leader of true genius. History has hardly known a man like him. Men were prepared to go to their graves for Frederick. Brave men. We are talking about a leader who could inspire armies. Oh well, it is our misfortune to have lived through these times and not his.'

Beenken sighed. Thomas knew all too well about his affections for the military. Beenken in fact went to great lengths to present himself as if from military stock, an ex-soldier perhaps, steeped in the histories and decorum

35

of army life. But in truth he'd never worn a uniform and not a single one of the medals he spoke of was his own – most of them had been bought from pawnbrokers when inflation hit veterans hard. The fact was, his kinship with the military was more wishful thinking than fact, and those who visited his room above Thomas' were invariably surprised by the lack of decorum in the furnishings, the shabbiness of its appearance and how his belongings amounted to little more than a pile of rubbish.

Beenken's three grey teeth propped up a smile. 'The next time this country goes to war, it will be under another Frederick, and we will have a new generation to go to battle.' With this comment he smirked, almost childishly.

'I'm not a soldier,' Thomas objected. 'I've no appetite to kill another person.'

'We are all soldiers – wouldn't you fight for your country?'

'I would do all I could to make friends with the enemy,' Thomas replied.

'My dear boy, now I know you're pulling my leg. After all, your country is all you have. Without it you are nothing.'

'I'd like to make my own choice about that.'

'Oh yes, of course – it's your life. That is why I respect you. But remember this: a man's country is his most important unit of identity. I will say no more on the matter.' Beenken adjusted his parting again and took on a self-satisfied look. 'I say boy,' he began again. 'Have you seen my flag? Oh yes, my family has its own standard; I take it whenever I go on visits.' Thomas laughed to himself; he knew Beenken never visited anywhere. 'And it will pass on from my generation to the next when I die. But you mustn't think of me in a different light just because I have my own flag. No, I wouldn't allow it. I have to earn your respect. Does that sound strange to you? That I should have to earn your respect? Well, it shouldn't. I would not deserve it otherwise. After all, we must never forget, a General is only as powerful as the allegiance of his men…'

Beenken looked about pensively for a moment. Thomas felt sure the old man was losing his sanity, especially when he swung from one dubious story to another, as he did next (and he was on particularly good form that day). 'I'm thinking of buying a cow, Thomas. An English breed I think. I'll put her out to pasture on the grass behind the building and collect the milk each evening. What do you think of that? A good idea, yes? Then one day I will take her to the slaughter and feast on her for a whole year. You must let me know if you want any meat, before it all runs out.'

Beenken turned away distracted and muttered to himself a few words, then taking babyish steps, as if his balance might just falter, or perhaps longing for a mother's arms to cradle him, he left the room.

Thomas breathed a sigh of relief. He got up and put away his new linen, then went to the window that overlooked the small patch of land to the rear of the building. He pictured a cow tethered there nibbling the scraps of grass, this rough square of dirt surrounded by trees and a brick wall on one side. During the day local residents would walk through the square; schoolchildren came and went in the afternoon. By twilight groups of older men populated the two benches, usually the shopkeepers, the grocers and the booksellers. The old men were later usurped by a series of night time revellers who arrived and left without pattern, drinking beer and singing.

From then on the area fell quiet, but if one listened

carefully one could hear the sing-song giggles of tipsy young couples among the trees. And when the noises were particularly expressive, Thomas would look out of his window and try to locate their shadows. At the same time, he would invariably hear the creak of floorboards above him and would know that Beenken was also looking out of his window over the same square of dirt, their eyes occupied by the same trembling darkness.

Just then, the old walrus put his head back through the doorway. 'Yes, yes, I knew there was something else. I forgot to mention. You've got a new roommate. I'll bring him by tomorrow if you don't mind. You don't mind do you?'

Thomas glowered. 'A new roommate? My rent covers this whole apartment! I'm not prepared to share. Not for a minute.'

Beenken shrugged his shoulders. 'I'm just telling you what I've heard. A new roommate for Thomas. That's what I've been told.'

'I won't stand for it!'

'The boy's name is Malik. It's been decided. That's the way things are I suppose.' Beenken shrugged again, withdrew his head and closed the door behind him.

THE SEARCH

"Be sure your sin will find you out" – Bible: Numbers

7

Potsdam City borders the southwest region of Berlin. As one heads along the River Havel, the water opens out into the Greater Wannsee Lake where the space unfurls and the air brightens. On summer days the beach fills with day-trippers from the capital and the blue lake plays host to the peaked white canvas sails of amateur boats.

Thomas did not travel according to the caprice of the river however, but rode by train to Potsdam, direct and at speed. On his way, he took a detour to the nearby town of Drewitz, where Orenstein and Koppel had its locomotive factory. If the thief-boy had worked there as he claimed, then it might be worth asking a few questions.

There was a vivid brightness to the day, where the light from the blue sky turned every building into a crystalline diamond. Thomas approached the factory, which stood on its own in a wide plane of industrial wasteland. It was surrounded at a distance by the stout silhouettes of other factory plants, whose chimneys burnished the open sky with columns of thick grey smoke. Had the thief-boy once walked this same dusty track towards the factory, as he did today?

Thomas went to the perimeter gate and entered without anyone stopping him. A hand-painted sign stated, 'Welcome to the circus' – the meaning of which

41

became apparent when he saw the workshop ahead of him, a large circular structure that had the look of a circus big-top.

He crossed the forecourt, which was brimming with the forms of half-finished locomotives, of wheels, pistons, connecting rods and cogs, strewn like the rocks of some abandoned ruins. He was about to go into the main workshop when he was called from behind by a stocky gentleman in lederhosen breeches and a domed hat.

'Can I help you?' he enquired.

Cautious not to reveal his real intentions, Thomas offered a made-up story to explain his presence. 'I am here on behalf of the *Berliner Tageblatt*,' he said. 'I'm a journalist. I've come to speak to some of your finest workers.'

'We're not expecting any journalists here,' the man said. He appeared to be in charge of the comings and goings of the factory, some sort of foreman.

'That's not my understanding,' Thomas insisted. 'I've been told that this factory is one of Berlin's greatest achievements. It has survived the most testing part of the decade.'

He fished around in his jacket pocket and pulled out his ID card for the *Berliner Tageblatt*. He was certainly no journalist; his ID card permitted him access only to the newspaper print rooms. Yet a brief flash of the card seemed to satisfy the man in lederhosen.

'It's been a difficult time for the factory,' the man confirmed, 'but we've come through it, stronger in my opinion.' His voice shifted to a more assertive tone, as if he was taking responsibility himself for the success of the factory.

Thomas knew his story of being a journalist had worked. 'Go on,' he encouraged, taking a pencil from his pocket as if about to make notes.

The foreman hooked his fingers into the straps of his lederhosen. 'We used to build engines and carriages for the government, to support the war and all that. But since then, our export markets have been blocked and the government is no longer taking orders. We had to close the entire factory for three months in '25, but things have picked up since then.'

'What about the men's morale? Have you had to lay many off?'

'Some. Back in the hardest times. Much less so in the past year.'

'And these men, where are they now? The ones who have left, do you ever hear from them again?'

'Not so much. The occasional man returns looking for work.'

Thomas was tempted to ask about the boy. Could he know something?

'Do you have many younger men here? Teenagers, I mean?'

The man in lederhosen was unsure about the line of questioning. His eyes narrowed. 'Perhaps you'd like to look around,' he said, failing to address Thomas' question. 'Follow me, if you like?'

'Thank you,' Thomas replied. 'Actually, I've been here before. Several times, in fact. I know my way around. I wouldn't want to distract you from your work.'

'I better take you.'

'No, it's not necessary. I'll just make my way through here.' Thomas pointed ahead. There were two long brick buildings with sliding shutter doors, and between them, a testing track that ran up to the main circus workshop. 'I know my way from this point,' he said, already walking away.

He took himself quickly into the workshop. It wasn't

43

obvious what he was looking for, but he felt satisfied to have made it this far. Orenstein and Koppel was open for business in Drewitz. That was one thing he now knew for certain.

The first thing he noticed inside the workshop was the temperature. The air was thick with a humid, pulsing heat that seemed to steal his breath away for a moment. And then there was the noise, the sound of hammer-blows against metal, winches being cranked and furnaces being stoked. Men glowing with dusty brown sweat did their work in a slow but relentless fashion. None of them looked up as Thomas passed through.

He found an adjacent office room with large glass windows. Inside he could see stacks of drawers and a large writing desk with papers all across it. He checked there was no one around, then he went in and closed the door.

He moved quickly, scouting the four corners of the office room with darting eyes. He approached the desk and, one-by-one, opened and closed the four sliding drawers that lined the front. Inside each was the debris of a badly organised stationery store, with pens and pencils, tape, wires, scissors, metal thumbtacks and an assortment of ink pots crammed messily in no particular order. On top of the desk were invoices and credit notes, along with a series of 'Orenstein & Koppel' company stamps.

He looked across the room. There was a typewriter with headed paper already loaded into the carriage and a bookcase with ledger books from floor to ceiling. He found two baskets for incoming and outgoing mail, which he rummaged through but found nothing of interest. Next, he moved to the tall stack of drawers behind the desk. It was only when he looked up and saw a photograph hung high on the wall above the drawers that he realised he had found what he was looking for.

The photograph showed a row of men sat on top of a trolley car. There were fifteen men in all. Some wore hats, some grasped the braces that held up their trousers, others smoked or crossed their arms or clutched one another around the shoulder. The photograph was dated 1927. Mounted on the wooden frame was a brass plaque with all the names of those depicted.

Thomas peered at the photograph. He moved from left to right, surveying every face. It was grainy and hard to focus. And yet, finally, right in the centre, he found the face of the boy. His beard was shorter, as was his hair, but the wire-rimmed glasses were just the same. Thomas cross-referenced with the brass plate and located the boy's name. A Hiller.

That was him. Now he had his name.

8

Käthe Hiller walked out onto the roof terrace and for ten minutes looked down to the city below, trying to spot her guest walking along the street. She arranged a chair on the left side where the view over the city was best. She put two cushions beneath her and a footstool nearby, drank coffee in the sun and opened a magazine on her knee. It was her monthly copy of *Revue de Monats*. On the front cover, a young woman held a champagne flute; inside there was an article on 'The Lives of the Rich and Beautiful on the Italian Riviera.'

Bells rang out across Potsdam. Above the rooftops toward the Breite Strasse, the Nikolaikirche played a chorale peal every half-hour. The church of Peter and Paul at the Bassinplatz chimed a pitch higher, with a melody in two parts at the beginning of every hour. From the Dutch quarter, chimes came frequently and washed over the terrace at intervals through the morning and afternoon.

Käthe didn't own the apartment herself. It belonged to her aunt Erika. Aunt Erika had big dark eyes crowded by wrinkles, and a large wart on her chin that, somehow, made her seem more beautiful. Käthe loved her aunt, all the more because she hardly ever saw her. Wasn't there something generous in the way aunt Erika never came around except when she knew Käthe would be out? It made Käthe feel the apartment was all her own, giving her the liberty to come and go by her own schedule, to hang her own pictures – not hesitating to bang nails into the walls – decorate the rooms with indoor plants and bake her own bread laced with imported black olives.

And when she looked out from the terrace, it was *her* view over Potsdam. With its chest-high iron balustrade, combined with its exceptional loftiness, the terrace had the feeling of some cathedral rooftop, teetering on the very fulcrum of the wind and sky. Then, when the orchestra of bells fell silent, a new set of sounds gradually took their place; the rumble of horse carts and motorcars eight floors below.

The morning was the liveliest time of all. She liked to lean forward and peer down, and watch the shopkeepers mop their steps and lift their shuttered blinds. There were also the young delivery boys from the butchers and bakers who weaved along the street with wicker baskets over their shoulders, and the servants from the big households rushing to do their daily errands. Then there was the postman with his leather satchel who rubbed shoulders with the bankers and clerks under narrow-rimmed hats, and the white-socked school children garnished with yellow neckerchiefs. Later came the shoe-shiners, tobacconists, policemen, students and soldiers on day-release. It felt like the whole world was here.

Then, at the end of the day, when the last wisp of yellow sunlight threaded through the sky and the red-tiles of the rooftops blushed peach, the city between the low hills, punctuated by the spires and domes of Protestant Germany, was cast in shadow, and Potsdam town, the second Versailles of Europe, prepared for sleep.

A few miles to the northeast lay the great metropolis of Berlin. Here was a city that smouldered all through

47

the night. Soot-encrusted, charged by electricity, Berlin was a place of music cafés, bars and theatres, where the streets purred with pleasure-seeking, where young women were watched by their admirers, where rakes, tarts, actors, composers and journalists – the whole menagerie – emerged, restless and newly eager.

Potsdam's ornaments were shadowed like faded pearls compared to Berlin's neon advertisements. The manicured gardens of the royal parks with their greenhouses of tropical fruit, trellised gazebos, a Chinese teahouse and a Turkish mosque, these all fell quiet across Postdam. Only the church bells kept watch over the hours, mournful in the mysteries of the night. At the same time, Berlin's pulse began beating harder and faster. Nightclubs opened, jazz music murmured and wailed, lovers found each other in the shadows.

Käthe had long felt attracted to Berlin's restless streets. It fascinated her, this almost mythical place that had gained such notoriety elsewhere in Germany. Originally from a village outside of Düsseldorf, she moved away to seek out a liveliness her hometown scarcely knew of. She came for the bars and coffeehouses, for the restaurants and cinemas, the shops and fashions – a treasury so inexhaustibly various she hardly wanted to spend another day without setting foot there.

Come morning in Potsdam, as the tallest church pinnacles caught the first streams of dawn light, the terrace began to light up again. Here Käthe sat with her coffee and magazine whose pages were filled with her waking dreams. She remembered as a child, there were days full of sunlight and wide-open spaces. She would do cartwheels over blades of grass, her head tumbling under her body, arms outstretched.

Standing up now, she put her hands on the railings

and leaned over, letting the breeze pass through her hair. She enjoyed the feeling as the sensation of vertigo took hold. In her mind she imagined how long it would take to fall such a distance, counting the numbers in her head, 1, 2, 3… Then she imagined what it would be like to be the object falling, tumbling through the air, uncontrollably towards the ground. She stepped back from the railings and took a breath. She felt alive with so many dangerous possibilities.

9

After Thomas had made his visit to the factory in Drewitz, he continued on to Potsdam. Once at the station, he walked directly to Käthe's apartment and climbed the staircase up to her door.

'Please come through to the living room,' she said as she answered, adopting a precise sort of politeness. She was carrying a magazine and wore an exhilarated look on her face. He watched her as she took the large bronze key she had used to unlock the front door and hung it in a wall-mounted key-box.

Once inside, he recognised the entrance hall with its carved dado-rail and painted Rosenthal vase. There were strips of eucalyptus-green wallpaper brightening one wall which continued into the bedroom, and in the corner there sat a rubber plant with over-sized leaves that lounged imperialistically. These lodgings had been scored in his memory more indelibly than he had realised.

'How have you been?' he asked.

'I'm well. I've been soaking in the view over Potsdam – and pondering Berlin too,' she said as she walked through the apartment. 'Your timing couldn't have been any better.'

He laughed gratefully and walked with her. She invited him to sit in one of the armchairs and suggested a small glass of apricot brandy for them both.

'Have you eaten?'

'I had my lunch in Berlin,' he said.

'You are so lucky to live there. I've always wanted to have an apartment in Berlin. I imagine it to be such a vibrant place.'

'Yes, but it has its drawbacks too.' He thought for a moment about Beenken and his rundown apartment, which was not a patch on hers.

'Would you take me for a night out?' she asked.

'In Berlin?' Thomas grinned, surprised. 'Yes, of course. I would love to. Would next Friday suit?'

'It would, thank you.' She smiled as she left the room to fetch the drinks. When she returned, she was without the brandy; instead she gave Thomas a glass of water and began searching the room, apparently looking for something lost.

'Is everything ok?'

'It's very odd. I seem to have mislaid something precious to me. My mother once gave me a small crystal decanter. I was going to serve your drink from it but I can't find it anywhere. It's a pretty, slender thing. She gave it to me for my eighteenth birthday. It's beautiful and worth something too.'

'Really?' Thomas sat up. 'When did you last see it?'

'I don't know. I remember cleaning it but that must have been a couple of weeks ago.'

He got up from his chair and began to look for the object himself, aware of the possibility that the thief may have taken it.

'Please, Thomas, sit down. I'm sure it will show up.'

He went to take a sip from his glass of water and found his hand was twitching. As he lifted the glass to his lips, he knew his throat would refuse to swallow.

'Perhaps someone has stolen it,' he stammered.

'Do you think so? But who would do that? I've only

51

had friends here.'

'It's possible. Maybe someone broke in.' He couldn't seem to stop himself.

She listened. Her mind went back to the newspaper she read on her lunch break at work, *Tempo*, which often gave police reports of criminals recently arrested or else details on unsolved crimes. If you believed the press, there were thieves and murderers around every corner. Perhaps there were?

'Don't say that,' she replied to Thomas' suggestion.

He realised he was alarming her. 'Then it could have been your landlord. My landlord is something of a scoundrel too. I wouldn't put it past him to help himself and take things of mine.'

'But this apartment belongs to my aunt. She would never steal from me. I suppose she might have just borrowed it. Perhaps she thought nothing of it and was hoping to return it without me realising.'

Thomas agreed with her, but deep down he knew she wasn't right. The thief must have taken the decanter; it must have gone over the side of the roof terrace along with him.

He pictured himself searching at the foot of the building, just as before, scouring the floor where a decomposing layer of manure, newspapers and vegetable scraps had gathered; and up above, the faint presence of the roof terrace, its black iron railings just about visible. Then he imagined seeing something among the filth, a shard of crystal poking through like a piece of gold panned from a muddy river. Surely a drop from such a height would shatter almost anything?

'It will turn up,' Käthe said, deciding to forget about the decanter. She suggested they went out to the terrace. 'It's so bright out today,' she said. 'I spent the whole morning out there.'

The high embankment of the terrace was just the same, an outcrop of brick amid the surrounding patchwork of roof tiles. A thin haze temporarily veiled the sky above, a shifting gauze which lent the terrace a firmer, more durable quality by contrast. The network of streets below appeared even further removed like a separate world.

'You are fortunate to have this view. Most fortunate,' Thomas said, shaking away his doubts over the decanter.

'So long as I can afford the rent, I will stay here,' she replied. 'My aunt is kind, she doesn't ask for much.' She sat down, thinking how lucky she was to be able to live there. To her mother, the idea of a single women renting an entire apartment was unthinkable. How long would her aunt keep the rent so low? She had no idea.

'Did you enjoy yourself last week?' Thomas asked. 'When the artist was here? It was fun, wasn't it?'

She thought back to the gathering of new friends in her apartment, which made her feel warm and more deeply embedded in her new life. The small country town where she grew up was happily receding in her memory, little by little. 'It was a wonderful day,' she said.

'You made for an excellent model.'

'Do you think so? I didn't know I could hold still for so long.'

'I was watching you.'

'Really? And were you impressed?' she asked, looking at him suggestively.

'Very.'

There was a long pause between them, a warm comfortable silence.

'Have you known Fräulein Constein for very long?' Käthe eventually said.

Thomas explained that he had known the artist for merely a fortnight.

'I understand she's a rising artist,' Käthe confirmed, admitting that she had never seen her work before, but like Thomas, 'had heard great things.'

Just then, beneath one of the foldaway chairs that had been left out on the terrace from the week before, Thomas noticed something glinting. A ray of sunlight reflected back from this single point on the floor. He rose up and he went over, expecting to find a shard of the missing decanter. He reached beneath the chair and instead picked up the lens from a pair of glasses. The wire-frame lay twisted nearby, with its second lens missing. He knew the glasses straight away. They belonged to the boy-thief.

He thought for a moment about hiding them from Käthe, but it was already too late. She came towards him and asked what he had found.

'A pair of glasses. They're broken.' Then he said faintly, 'Do you know who they belong to?'

She took the lens and frame from him and turned the pieces over in her fingers. She began levering the hinges. To his surprise, she responded immediately.

'These are my brother's.'

'You have a brother?'

'Yes. His name is Arno. These are his glasses.'

'Arno? Arno Hiller?'

'That's right.'

'I didn't know you had a brother,' Thomas said, his voice quick and startled.

'He's younger than me. By seven years, nearly eight. These are his glasses. But I don't understand how they got here. He hasn't been here in months.'

'Then you're sure they're his?'

'I'm certain. Look, they're engraved with his initials.'

She eased back one of the arms and pointed to a tiny engraving near to the lens. It read A. H.

Thomas thought back to the photo he'd seen at the factory. A pall of dread swept across him. 'But if he hasn't visited?'

'He sometimes comes over. He likes to drop in spontaneously. He has his own key you see, so he must have visited. But why his glasses are broken and left like this, I don't know.'

Käthe wandered towards the terrace railings, her mind sifting through the puzzle.

At the same moment, the worst of thoughts crystallised in Thomas' head, that her younger brother and the vagrant thief-boy were one and the same person. Could Erich have mistaken him? Could they both have mistaken him for an intruder?

The chime of church-bells circled faintly. For the duration of a minute or two, they sounded in spiralling verse.

'Did your brother ever work in a factory?' he asked in one final attempt to disprove his worst expectations.

'Orenstein and Koppel?' she said.

'Yes, that's it.'

'Yes, for a few months. I'm not sure what happened. My parents told me he left there. How do you know about Orenstein and Koppel?'

'Oh, I don't know. Just a guess. I heard a lot of people who come to Berlin work there.'

'The factory is not far from here. In Drewitz, I believe.'

Thomas took a sharp breath as the pieces began to fall into place. It had to be her brother, not a thief at all, but a young man with every right to be there. He must have been the stranger who approached them in the bar. A chance meeting – and not a down-and-out at all, but Käthe's brother. Erich had taken retribution on an innocent boy. It was just like the story Erich had told, about the missing soldier, struck down when he entered his own home.

Thomas turned away from Käthe as the terror of the coincidences multiplied in his mind. He couldn't look at her. He was horrified by his own part in the event.

Then the mist above the terrace shifted and opened, and sunlight penetrated the terrace like a silver blade, casting everything into shadows and relief. Now the buildings around, the brick, the concrete, the street below, the metal and rubber of motorcars, the trams and bicycles and the sounds of the city, all of these things seemed to gather up, sharpen and tighten around him. A bitter taste entered his mouth as his throat constricted.

'You must tell me if you hear from your brother,' he said. 'If you hear from him, you must tell me immediately.'

'Are you ok?' she asked. 'What's the matter?'

'I'm not sure.'

'Is it the height? Do you want to go inside?'

'Yes. Only, I have the strangest feeling. This terrace...'

She led him back through to the living room. She was still holding the pair of glasses. Thomas sat in one of the armchairs and felt a sour embarrassment rising in him. What would she think? Would he always have this rancid response every time he set foot on the terrace? But – he knew too well – these were the least of his worries.

'I might take a walk if you don't mind. A breath of fresh air will do me good.' He looked over and realised he didn't want to be in her company in that instant.

'Shall I come with you?'

'No, no. I'll go downstairs and take a walk up the street. I'll contact you about Berlin next week. I promise. But I must go now.'

He moved past her and went quickly to the front door. The next moment, he was stood on the street at the base of the building, thankful for the hard cobblestones beneath his feet. He breathed deeply and found the air to be fogged with the solid scents of tobacco and car fumes. The whole awful secret was too poisonous to share. Arno! He had been punished for nothing!

He slipped away along the street, smuggling himself back to the train station, and as he went, he resolved to confront Erich with the truth at the very next opportunity.

10

The May elections saw the city coated in political posters pasted onto any unclaimed brick wall or unmanned kiosk. The hammer-and-sickle emblem of the Communists fought for attention with the swastika of the Nazis. Agitators from both sides rallied against the filth and decadence of Berlin, each promising that the future would be golden under their reign. When all the walls were sufficiently covered, motorcars and omnibuses were fitted with great placards big enough to carry two-dozen more posters on either side. These vehicles could be seen roving and weaving through the city at walking pace. On their roofs, men stood and bawled out to passersby. The socialists would declare 'Red unity across city and countryside!' whilst the fascists would claim 'My honour is called loyalty!'

As Thomas ventured out that afternoon he saw a huge parade of Communists surging along the street. It could be heard before it was seen: brass trumpets and tubas played a marching tune with snare drums leading the charge. Banners and great red flags jostled in the air above the heads of hundreds of men in Bolshevik caps like an army of Lenins descending on the city. After them came the women and children, some decked out in neckerchiefs and carrying yet more flags, which when the wind caught their sails, billowed out and revealed the face of Stalin, Trotsky or else Rosa Luxemburg.

The street soon became impassable due to the crowds, and Thomas found himself stood next to a bank clerk in a suit smoking a cigarette. The clerk glanced at Thomas and let out a plume of smoke. 'They dream of storming the Reichstag like they stormed the Winter Palace in Petrograd,' the man said. 'This is another fight that us Germans must not lose.'

'Another fight?' Thomas asked.

'Germany never lost in the war. Didn't you realise that? Not a bit of it. We were betrayed by the socialists and Jewish weasels. They signed away what was never theirs to begin with. That's what these fools don't understand. The working people of this country should have a promise of the rightful share of the German rebirth, once the dictate of Versailles is overturned.'

'You mean a share of the land?'

'I mean *national* socialism. Men have a right to know their country is pure-blood. No more clandestine Jews dominating from the shadows. And certainly no more Communists with their red ribbons. Give me jackboots and military insignia any day. We need discipline and loyalty. Not this motley gang of Soviet philosophers.'

The bank clerk trod on his cigarette and moved away. Thomas watched the rally for a while longer. For some reason, he thought back to his first years in Berlin, back in 1921, when he came and started to make a life for himself in the metropolis. The war was still a recent memory. If you wanted to, you could buy guns and ammunition practically everywhere. A steady trickle of Mauser rifles – the same model 98 used by the army – returned to the city and began appearing on market stalls and in the windows of shops that didn't care to hide them. War casualties sat twisted on every street corner, some of them real, others undoubtedly fake. The fakes were easier to spot because they exaggerated everything – they shook and convulsed when you walked by, then fell asleep again once you had passed. The genuine veterans did their best to earn your respect: they offered you chocolate in exchange for some coins, or they tried to sing or just clap their hands if they couldn't hold a tune. It was desperate and depressing and perfectly familiar all at the same time.

Then inflation spun out of control. The mark began to tumble against foreign currencies, slow at first but every day getting faster. At its worst, people would bring briefcases of banknotes to the butchers just to buy a rasher of bacon. Thomas remembered how it used to be, getting paid and then dashing over the bridge to reach the food shops before two o'clock – at which time the mark was devalued again and the blackboards were chalked-up with new prices.

On the street before him, the Communist rally rolled on. Thomas noticed the tail end of the march, dozens of urchin children following in tow. They were laughing and skipping in time to the parade's music.

And then the mêlée began: a quartet of Nazi thugs carrying truncheons and metal rods dashed towards the column of the demonstration and began to clout as many Communists as they could before they were pounced on. Within seconds, fists were smashing into faces and arms were clasping around necks. Wounded men staggered away with blood dripping from their heads. The music kept playing its jaunty rhythm as the street brawl waxed and waned.

As for the urchin children, they had long since fled like mice scattering from sight. The bloodshed made Thomas feel like doing the same.

He managed to make his way in the opposite direction.

His primary intention that day was to find a doctor's surgery and ask for an impromptu appointment. As luck would have it, the local practice was still open.

'I can't find anything wrong with you,' the doctor said, growing impatient by Thomas' persistence.

'But can't you do more tests?' Thomas asked. 'These dizzy spells are not usual for me.'

The doctor threaded himself into a long charcoal-grey overcoat, single-breasted, with six large black buttons arranged in rows on the front. Thomas had taken the last appointment of the day; now the doctor had to rush off for his wife's birthday.

'As far as I can tell, you're in perfect health,' the medic said as he buttoned up his coat. With his trilby hat and necktie he appeared smart and sombre, yet a pair of blue velvet gloves gave his look an uncommon verve. 'Try to rest. See how you feel in a week or two,' he said.

Thomas nodded. 'Okay, I'll try to relax. Oh, before you go, could you answer me one more thing? It's an odd question I know, but have you ever dealt with a fall?'

'A fall? Of course. A broken leg, a shattered elbow.' The doctor rubbed his gloved hands together. His mind was turning to his wife and whether she would like the silver necklace he'd bought for her.

'What about a fall from a height?' Thomas asked. 'Have you ever seen somebody fall from a great height?'

'I once treated someone after they tumbled out of a third floor window.'

'Really? And did they survive?'

'A broken leg as I recall. Nothing more serious. In my opinion they were lucky.'

'And how high do you think the window was?'

'How high was the window? I really couldn't tell you. What's your purpose here?'

'I'm curious, that's all. I don't mean to be rude.

Perhaps you could tell me this: have you ever seen somebody fall from a height of say, seven or eight floors?'

'Seven or eight? It depends on the conditions. Onto what surface?'

'What about onto cobblestones?'

'These are not the sort of questions I normally... I suppose you'd have to be exceptionally lucky.'

'But it's possible?'

'To survive? Of course, anything is possible.'

'You really think somebody could survive?'

'No, I don't. I'd say it's extremely unlikely. But not impossible. Herr Strack, what is the meaning of your questions?'

Thomas shook his head. 'It's hypothetical, that's all.'

'Please, get some rest. I must go home to my wife now. Come back to me in a fortnight if you haven't improved.'

As Thomas left the surgery he considered his next choice. He could make a trip to the mortuary to see if they'd recently added the body of Arno Hiller to their vaults. He also thought of searching through the wards at Potsdam's main hospital in case Arno was an inpatient there. His third thought was to go to the police and somehow fish for news of a possible murder case. Instead, he approached a line of newspaper-sellers with the evening editions pegged to their chests and bought a copy of every paper on display.

He returned to his apartment with his bundle of newspapers and spent the next hour scouring through the pages on the lookout for a death notice or an obituary or anything else that might hint at the disappearance of Arno Hiller. He discovered that plenty of people had died or been attacked across the city, but none of them answered to the description of the boy in the wire-rimmed spectacles.

With newspapers strewn all over the floor, he paced back and forth. Just then, he heard his door unlock, and into the room came a strange young man.

'You must be Thomas,' the new arrival stated loudly.

'And you must be my new roommate,' Thomas said, perfectly begrudgingly.

The young man stepped forward and shook Thomas' hand.

'Oh yes. That is I. My name is Malik – Malik the Orphan. You may have heard me shouting across the city. I'm in utter shock. All I have to say is this: it is a disgrace to our society!'

Thomas began gathering up the newspapers from the floor. 'A disgrace? What happened to you?'

'I was left on the street to rot like a dead rat. My last landlord washed his hands of me. I was a month or two behind in my payments. So what? There are worse crimes out there, you know?' He pointed out through the window, then advanced to tell a lengthy tale of how his fortunes had turned upside down thanks to the venal-minded city. It was a sorry tale, and yet the boy seemed wholly invigorated by the turn of events. His large circular face held a big set of grinning teeth, which appeared to be bursting out of his mouth, offering a picture of surest happiness. He was one of the oddest people Thomas had ever met.

The boy fumbled through his pockets and pulled out a bent cigarette, then in an amateurish way, gripped the cigarette between his large teeth, lit a match and began to smoke it. His appearance reminded Thomas of a child dressed up in adult clothing. Like Beenken, there was something of the actor in him, and something of the innocent schoolboy too. He smoked as if he'd never smoked before in his life. He didn't appear to enjoy the experience as the first puff was followed by a coughing fit that he tried his best – but failed – to contain.

'How long will you stay?' Thomas asked, somewhat intrigued by his new youthful companion. Perhaps having a new roommate wouldn't be so bad after all.

'Who can tell?' the boy beamed. 'I am the victim of a tremendous injustice, that's the only thing I know for certain. How can a young man like me make it on my own, out there? The world prefers corrupt men, which means I maybe destined for a life with the cats. Thank God for people like you and Herr Beenken.'

Malik began unpacking his belongings across one side of the apartment: a small collection of books, including volumes by Nietzsche, a heavy fur-lined overcoat, a silver wristwatch, a newspaper called *Die Rote Front*, and a tea set made of English porcelain. As he set out his things, he talked about being a student at the university. Thomas noted the broad range of his interests, everything from Buddhism to boxing. For Malik, the great metropolis presented itself like a diamond with endless facets. 'This city has enough life to fill a million novels,' he said. 'Tragedies most of them. But let us act now and reflect later. That's what my dear mother used to say, anyway. Now, onto important matters. I want to give you this.' A hand came forward holding a business card of some sort. 'Why don't you come to one of our meetings?'

Thomas read the card: *Roter Frontkämpferbund – Alliance of Red Front-Fighters*. 'So you're a Communist are you?' he concluded.

'There are some extraordinary people out there. The most original thinkers. I'm intrigued by new ideas and I hate old ideas just as strongly.'

'Is that so? I've always treated politics with a healthy pinch of salt,' Thomas replied. Whenever he thought about the contending forces – the Communists, the Nazis, and the shambles of a government – his first thought was to tear up his ballot paper.

'You must come along some day,' Malik said.

'I was there today, in fact. I watched the rally march through Potsdamerplatz. It ended in a street brawl, of course.'

'There's to be another meet-up outside Berlin Cathedral next week,' Malik responded, adding with a sparkle, 'there is sure to be violence there too.'

'Are you a member?'

'I'm looking into it. Except, one has to proclaim an oath to join the movement.'

'Then you'd best decide if you truly believe, especially if you have to fight for the cause.'

'Oh I'm willing to fight,' the boy replied. 'But that's enough about me, tell me something interesting about yourself.'

Thomas responded by telling Malik about his part in Jana Constein's painting. 'There is much talk about her in the Berlin Academy, and I'm going to be in one of her compositions.'

Malik's face fell. 'A painting?' he pondered. 'I'm not sure I approve.'

'How do you mean? How could you disapprove?'

'It is very simple. Paintings are part of bourgeois culture. Your so-called work of art is a one-off. It is unique. Probably it is very expensive, therefore it is elitist. It is out of the reach of most working people. That's why I must disapprove.' He stepped forward and said, rather triumphantly, 'Cinema! Cinema is the thing! Cinema is the art that will replace painting. Cinema can be multiplied and taken across the world. You can take your easel paintings and burn them as far as we are concerned.'

65

'So all of painting is dismissed, just like that?'

Malik's thick smile beamed and his eyes swelled. He pointed at the card still in Thomas' hand. 'If you believe in the future, you will join us. I can tell you are looking for something to do with your life. Where is your calling Thomas? I know you are homeless at the moment.'

'Homeless? I'm not the one who's homeless.'

'Intellectually I mean. You are without an intellectual home.'

'That's not true.'

'Please, don't take offence. All I mean is, you cannot put it off forever. It's time to find your calling. You are getting older. How many years older than me are you?'

'I don't know. Ten years. Maybe more.'

'It doesn't matter Thomas. They're just numbers. The point is, you're are still young; you still have time. The best thing you can do for yourself is to join a group like ours. I was sleeping before I became interested in ideas of fraternity – how I have woken up since! I have found my vocation, and even if that lousy slug who threw me out into the street like a piece of dirty meat, even if snakes like him are around every corner, well they will only make me more determined. That is my vocation. To protect the friend, to fight off the enemy!'

'Perhaps I will come. Another day,' Thomas said.

'I am sure you will find the idea of utopia quite appealing,' Malik said as he flopped onto his bed and promptly fell asleep.

Thomas felt a shudder of recognition at Malik's words, *to protect the friend, to fight off the enemy*. A mist of visions passed before his mind, of Erich and the roof terrace and Arno Hiller. Surprised at how at ease he felt in the presence of his new roommate, Thomas suddenly had the urge to speak about the events in Potsdam. Could Malik's unique perception throw some light on them? He went over to Malik's bed and shook him by the shoulder. Two eyes opened and a grin widened.

'Listen to me,' Thomas said.

Malik roused himself as Thomas laid out the story of the roof terrace and the thief-boy. The only thing he left out was the notion of who the boy might in fact be.

'And you found no body?' Malik questioned, nodding his head with overdone sensitivity. He seemed to enjoy being confided in.

Thomas confirmed the absence of the body.

'What time did this all happen?'

'It was about six in the morning. Yes, exactly six. I remember the church bells ringing.'

'So you had been drinking and were up all night?'

'Yes, but I remember everything clearly.'

'You *think* you remember it clearly.'

'I do, and when we went down to search for the boy there was no body to speak of,' Thomas exclaimed.

'Let me understand this correctly. You say a thief broke into your girlfriend's apartment?'

'She's not my girlfriend.'

'But you are fond of her? Quite obviously you are.'

'That's not relevant.'

Malik eased into a smirk. 'You say a thief broke into an apartment belonging to a beautiful woman? Then you say you wanted to tie him up for revenge.'

'Not revenge. And I didn't say she was beautiful.'

'I'm getting awfully confused,' Malik said. 'Is she not beautiful then?'

'Yes, but the point is…'

'The point is that she is a beautiful woman. Why deny it? Thomas, relax. I've known beautiful women.'

'Is that so?'

'Yes indeed. I was once engaged to a beauty from Hamburg… Ah, but that is another story. So you say, you went to get some rope to tie him with?'

'Yes.'

'And then, when you returned, you say you saw your friend – Erich was it? – push him over the railings? And he fell? He fell down to the ground?'

'Yes. That's exactly what I saw.'

'You saw him hit the ground?'

'No, but he fell from the other side of the railings. There is no other conclusion.'

'Does your friend deny it?'

'No. He accepts it. He is proud. He believes in the experience of such things.'

'He is proud? He is proud of depraved actions? Is he a monster?' Malik shook his head moralistically.

'He believes justice has been served but he doesn't understand the full implications.'

'Then I would say your friend is guilty in the most emphatic terms,' Malik pronounced. 'I know how cruel this world is. Thank God for men like you, who at least show some degree of conscience. Criminality must be punished. You must see to it that your friend gets what he deserves.'

'Then I should report him?'

'Immediately.'

'Then I will be guilty. Of betrayal. Besides, I still have no proof.'

'Proof? You have your own eyes. That should be proof enough.'

Thomas listened to Malik's certainty and felt himself convinced by it. He went to the printing rooms of the *Berliner Tageblatt* that night fixated on new concerns, for he felt sure he had to confront Erich. By the morning, as he returned home in the weak light of dawn, he knew what he had to do next.

11

Through the following week, Thomas went in pursuit of Erich. He travelled through the tunnels of the U-Bahn and paced along the wide boulevards of the Wilhelmstrasse and Leipzigerstrasse, dipping into bars and cafés, the places he knew Erich frequented to satisfy his appetites. Across the city, which seemed so huge and indifferent to his concerns, Thomas searched and searched. He went to the clubs where Erich was a member and visited his favourite entertainment establishments. On two separate occasions he telephoned Erich's parents. But there was no sign of his old friend no matter where he looked.

Then, by the time the weekend arrived, a new prospect was beginning to present itself. It was Friday, and the question of where he might take Käthe for a night out in Berlin had preoccupied him all afternoon. He had one idea, but dare he act on it?

He'd first been introduced to *The Cabaret of the Nameless* by an acquaintance from work. It was a smoky studio not far from Potsdamerplatz. The purpose of *The Cabaret of the Nameless* was to encourage the most inept performers onto the stage where their routine might be tried out at the pleasure of the paying customer. As entertainment went, it was a vicious sport. Genuinely talented performers were barred from performing and only the hopelessly amateurish allowed to enter, where they were cheered, jeered and glowered over.

Places like this were a reminder of the darker side of Berlin. Entertainment, spontaneity, theatre – yes, but there were other faces that represented the city just as well. Every so often a man with grotesque shrapnel-wounds would appear on the other side of the street, his face skewed pink by a war injury, or another veteran in a make-shift wheelchair pushing himself along with rags around his hands. Such images served to remind the rest of city how inglorious their foundations were. Beneath the pleasure seeking and the decadence there was a darker undercurrent to Berlin. There was social anxiety, poverty and the memory of a lost war. Then there were the endless political skirmishes, election posters everywhere, Communists threatening revolution, and the ever-present shadow of right-wing paramilitary groups like The Steel Helmet and the Young German Order, not to mention the Nazis.

In his apartment, Thomas went to his window. Malik had gone out for the night leaving him alone. He drew back the drapes and peered down to the street below. There he stayed for two or three minutes, a silent eyewitness to the antics of the busiest street in the city. He might have been watching from the shadowed hideaway of a private box in a theatre, his view over the street deliberately periphery. City noises rose up; car horns, tram bells, horses' hooves and high-heels. Substances of manufacture and industry, stone and steel, combined with the colourful enterprises of commerce and fashion, were abundant. The heritage of the previous century had not turned antique but had grown, blossomed and become symphonic. Berlin!

In the evenings, the wide boulevards simmered with candelabras – it was warm enough to enjoy a leisurely walk at this time of the year. There were lit-up shop fronts and waylaid strollers on their way to and from nightspots. Every week a new neon light was added to the skyline – *Kino*, *Parfüm*, *Schokolade* – promising yet more distraction. After the chastity of winter, it seemed that pleasure-seeking had been rediscovered. The springtime had given the city a fine prospect, animated and gregarious, as if the great energies stored up over the previous season could finally be let loose again. Thomas felt the changes too. He usually loved this time of year, the sparkle in the water and the light reflected in the glass of shop windows.

The noisy city rumbled through the walls. Had he been wrong? In his derision of the city was he not in fact paying tribute to it? Was not Berlin's instability part of its charm? After all, it was really much too large and too intricate to be summed up in a single derogatory thought.

He waited for another minute or two, taking in the bustle and rush of the street scene. Lines from the poet Baudelaire lodged in his imagination. *But evening comes, the witching hour, the uncertain light.*

Retreating like the daylight, he drew his curtains and turned on the lights. He had already cleaned from top to bottom the day before, and following that had arranged his few belongings into something that resembled a civilised existence. Carefully he chose a number of books from his shelf and made a small pile of them on the table with the Baudelaire on top. From the same shelf he removed a row of decaying china mugs and in their place propped up a framed reproduction of a painting by Renoir. It wasn't much to his taste, but it did add a dash of much-needed colour against the walls. He found a box of white candles in the building's storeroom and arranged three of them in candleholders around the room. The day before, he'd bought a fresh bar of soap, and earlier in the present day he fixed a broken floorboard with two well-positioned nails. Finally, he borrowed a Persian-style rug from a neighbour and laid it in the centre of the room. It was a musty rectangle of fabric, yet to his surprise when the evening light caught the turquoise and yellow patterns, the room lit up in a way it never had before.

He went to wash his hands, checked his fingernails, pulled down his shirt-sleeves and buttoned up the cuffs. He put on a brown tie, then after that a brown jacket. His shoes were already polished. He went to check himself in the mirror, listening out for a woman's footstep as if no event, before or since, had carried more significance. He looked every bit his thirty-two years. His eyes were bright and his complexion was pinched red as if flushed with a tropical heat. How could she fail to fall in love with him? His head was crowned with a broad wave of dark brown hair tamed from left to right with wax – like a flag flying across his brow. He was clean-shaven. His skin was smooth across his face and his sharp protrusive nose seemed especially elegant. In all, he felt very happy with his looks, and moreover, had the strange feeling that things would go the way he wished that evening.

He looked around his apartment once more, momentarily glancing towards the door, thinking he heard something. He was feeling clumsy and excited, giddy and powerful all at the same time. The wait was becoming too excruciating to bear. He left his apartment and went down the staircase.

As he did, he caught the aroma of the large bakery on the street below. The smell of warm bread seeped through the floorboards, Kümmelbrot, Sonnenblumkernbrot and the dark pumpernickel that had been cooking in steam chambers for a whole day. 'I

72

hope she likes bread,' he said to himself, emerging onto the evening street, ready to seize the night.

12

Under the glistening lamps of the Kurfürstendamm, Thomas saw the city in all its night time grandeur. He glanced into the restaurants as they filled up with friends and lovers. He stopped at the window of the F.V. Grünfeld department store with its slick chrome and glass frontage. The display was like a fizzing champagne glass full of light and bubbles.

At the same time, Käthe Hiller walked along the street with a confident stride. Her oriental-style strawberry-red shoes clapped the stone street as the gritty air of the city gently swept across her skin. She tried to remember how long she had waited to see the night scenes of Berlin. She was ready now, primed by an appetite that had been stirring for years. It was a need for something bigger, stranger, more wild – a feeling that her parents could never understand.

It had been nearly two weeks since she and Thomas met for the first time on the roof terrace. She recalled the manner of her own introduction – and smiled to herself as she thought back: 'My name is Käthe,' she had said. She held out her hand. 'I only shake hands when I meet somebody for the first time; next time we meet you can kiss me once on the cheek.'

She chuckled at her own words, which sounded so demure and formal in retrospect. What impression she was trying to make, she had totally forgotten.

Secretly she checked herself to make sure she appeared how she intended. She wore a stylish navy blue jacket with a purple thistle brooch pinned on the lapel. Her dress, white with blue bands, came down just below the knee, and was finished off with a polka dot scarf. And the new pair of red shoes, which had cost her a week's worth of wages, fitted perfectly well.

The man she had arranged to meet was already stood on the street corner, his hands lolling in his pockets. She saw him first. She liked that, being first to spot him, and the tiny advantage it gave her.

Thomas turned and, all of a sudden, she was there.

'Hello,' he said as she walked towards him. How finely dressed she was!

She shaded her eyes as a ray of evening sun dazzled her. 'Such a warm evening. I think it's pretending to be summer.' She drew her hair from her face and he gave her a kiss on the cheek.

'It will be summer before you know it,' he said. 'Did you have any problems finding your way?'

'I took the train and then the tram. It was easy.'

'So shall we find somewhere for a drink?'

'Yes, let's do that. Do you know the Romanische Café? I've heard that's where all the writers and actresses go. Will you take me there? We might bump into someone famous.'

'I've got other plans, if you don't mind?' Thomas replied.

'Wherever you think is best, but can I see where you live first? Is this the building?'

'You want to see inside? Why not? It's a bit spartan but it's comfortable.'

He led her through the wooden doors into the building. As they went inside, she told him a story about her neighbour's dog and how its barking had kept her awake all through the night. 'But,' she explained, 'just recently I was given a new radio set, and in the evening before bedtime, I always listen to some music. Whatever I can find on the dial. The other night I heard the most marvellous performance of Schubert. One of his symphonies, I don't know which one. I enjoyed it so much I wasn't ready to sleep, so I used the wretched dog as an excuse to stay up half the night and search for more music, though most of the time all I heard was crackle.'

'So you like music?'

'I like everything! Oh that reminds me – is there anywhere around here to dance? I love dancing.'

'There's a place not far from here. I've never been there before, but we can try it out. That's one thing about this city at night: if you want something, you can always find it.'

Together they climbed the stairs to the first floor. Just as they reached the top, Thomas spotted Herr Beenken slothfully descending from the floor above.

'Quickly,' he said. 'Let's get inside.' He grabbed Käthe's arm and pulled her towards his room. But it was too late. The sniffling old man called out and the pair were caught. Thomas introduced his companion.

'Very charming too,' Beenken said, sending a smile into the air. 'My wife,' he began, changing the subject immediately, 'has a silly idea she wants to visit Africa. That barbarian place. I can't think why. Can you explain it to me?' Thomas knew he was lying – Beenken didn't even have a wife. 'Is there not enough to see in this historic country?' Beenken asked.

Thomas began to pull on Käthe's arm again leading her off the landing, but Käthe was happy to stay and chat.

'You should never underestimate the lure of the exotic,' she said in the sort of cheerful tone Herr Beenken might approve of.

Indeed he did approve. His eyes widened as he steered his head in Käthe's direction. 'You are right, of course,' he said, delighted by his new acquaintance. 'You are certainly right, but still I won't let her go. The real challenge is to find the exotic on one's own doorstep.'

'Yes, I agree. Is your wife here this evening?' she asked.

'Oh no,' Beenken said confidently. 'She is singing in the theatre tonight. She has a role in a new play up town. Can't think of the name right now. But what a pretty woman she is. Only twenty years old! She lives on the second floor.' He pointed a meaty finger up towards the vacant room on the next floor up. Käthe glanced at Thomas, a confused look in her eye.

'We have to be going,' Thomas said.

'So soon? Well, yes, I suppose young love can't wait…' Beenken trailed off, only to start up again. 'Thomas? Do you remember Fräulein Gerlach?' Beenken suddenly took on a misty, romantic look. 'I took her to the spa town of Baden-Baden once for a romantic weekend? She had a beard, which was bad luck for her. Do you remember that amazing woman? Well, no, perhaps you don't. The two of us were lovers for a few months. The autumn of eighteen ninety-nine… Hah! You're surprised that I could love a woman with a beard, but my dear boy, she didn't have a beard when I knew her. Oh no, that only came much later. After I'd broken her heart. And do you remember the girl with the huge chest, Fräulein Benn? Probably you don't. That was years before you came to live with me. What a bosom it was! Shame I never got to see it in its full glory!' The look in Beenken's eyes glazed for a moment, and Thomas saw

77

his little grey turtle-tongue poke out between his teeth and wiggle in the light. 'They were marvellous women,' the old man went on. 'The sort of women one doesn't encounter these days. You are not alive in the good times boy. This country has seen better days.'

'Excuse me!' Käthe interrupted.

'Ah yes, ah yes. But there's still some beauty time can't steal, of course.'

'Time for us to go,' Thomas said, keen to make their exit.

'You're leaving. Yes, of course you are. But let me just say this to you Thomas: don't ask too much of your young friend here. Don't be too forward. She is pretty, so she will get men swarming around her all of the time. If you want to make an impression, take heed of my advice.'

Thomas feigned an appreciative smile.

'Are you listening to me? That is the smartest lesson I ever taught myself – how to love without expecting much in return. Then, my dear boy, life becomes extraordinarily rich. Falling in love is a pleasure that should be enjoyed as deeply as possible.'

Thomas stifled a growing frustration. 'We must be off. Goodnight Herr Beenken.'

'Aren't I going to see where you live?' Käthe asked.

'Another time.'

'Goodbye,' she called to Beenken.

'Goodbye my darling,' the old man called back.

Thomas winced.

The couple emerged back out onto the street, which seemed livelier now than before. They promenaded through the evening material, where people gathered and laughter bloomed. Lamp-lit frivolity seemed to lap around them from all directions. They found themselves caught up in numerous exchanges with strangers; fleeting glances and happy chit-chat. A young French couple asked them for directions to a hotel. A man with a patch over his eye and an enormous smile asked for money or anything they could spare. Then, all of a sudden, a party of Jewish socialites came tumbling out of a side door and for a minute swept the couple along with them. They were so delighted by the pair that they invited them to stay, eat and drink with them through the evening. Such attention made the new couple feel overwhelmingly convivial.

'Where is the dance hall? Is it near here?' Käthe asked. Thomas led the way with a breezy stride. When they arrived outside a gargantuan, gothic-looking building, they stopped to read the posters pasted on the wall: 'A Traditional Russian Evening,' Thomas read out loud. The pair looked at each other, laughed for no good reason, and then went inside. What they found they would never forget.

The hall was large and loud. Whatever was going on inside was already in full swing. At the front a small orchestra played, dominated by a banging drum that kept time to a chorus of violins and cellos. The music was loosely played and some of the violinists stood up and stamped to the rhythm. From the ceiling streamers hung, forming a multi-coloured canopy that stretched above the entire dance floor like the sky at sunset. The marching beat of the music made everything tremor. In the middle of the hall, a crowd of happy revellers kicked their legs and pounded their feet to the beat of the percussion.

Thomas' initial impression was that the whole thing was an orchestrated ball, an unruly mazurka, perhaps traditional to the people there. But on closer inspection he realised it was much too shambolic for that. It was more of an improvised custom, with the people making exaggerated movements and expressions, cajoling each other and enjoying the rumpus of the whole occasion. After a while the music seemed to reach a peak, where all the people roared out in chorus and the noise was deafening. Once the climax was overcome, a man who stood at the helm of the small orchestra, who wore an official-looking red uniform and seafaring-style hat, shouted out a phrase in what was presumably Russian. Then with a great gasping voice, waving his arms in circles, he encouraged the band to start up again. The musicians obliged, only this time louder and faster and more absurd than before. At this, the people cheered and went back to their dancing, laughing and slapping each other on their backs. It was quite a sight, unruly, extrovert and electrifying all at once.

Thomas and Käthe looked at each other on the edge of laughter and disbelief at this wild spirited soirée. Who were these people? Some clapped, some shouted and sang, it was like a frenzy without limit. Käthe put her hands over her ears and shook her head. They decided they would not stay long. There was something almost disheartening in the sham spectacle. Instead, they went back out onto the street and giggled and made fun of the strange dancers inside.

Käthe grabbed Thomas' hand and together they made a dash down the street, hyped up between them and almost tripping over in their jest. She led the way towards some people who had gathered up ahead, to what at first appeared to be a street performer with a crowd looking on. The performer wore a large tatty overcoat and was holding onto a broomstick, and was shouting energetically to the makeshift audience.

'Come forward, ladies and gentlemen,' he called. 'I want to welcome you into my travelling circus, a cabinet of wonder. You will not believe your senses! Come and

80

see our closet of curiosities.'

'What have you got?' came a shout from the crowd.

'My good man, we have a woman with three breasts!' At this, the small crowd laughed. 'But that is not all! We have the dwarfs! We have giants! Oh yes, and we have the man who has defied all of science – he is pregnant! But there is more!' Now the crowd exploded into exuberant shouting. Two young boys ran forward and pushed the circus man, knocking the broom out of his hand. Nobody knew what the broom was for. 'Clear off! Get away!' he shouted, then regaining himself, 'Now, ladies and gentlemen. We have unmentionable delights. Just come inside my tent. You'll see nothing less than the pickled brain of Napoleon Bonaparte!' The crowd burst into uproar again. The performer was clearly nothing but a bawdy charlatan. There was no tent to speak of.

At this point, another passer-by began shouting back at the entertainer, accusing him of deception and shamelessness. 'Where is your circus, you fool? You are a drunken madman! Go home.'

'My circus is through here,' replied the speaker, pointing to a brick wall behind him.

'There's nothing there,' replied the other man. 'Why don't you go back to the sewers? Leave this city.'

'Sewers? Did you hear that ladies and gentlemen? He called me vermin! No sir, I am a magician. I am the bearer of fantastic gifts.'

'You bring pollution! You are polluting this city.'

'I do nothing of the sort. I tantalise the senses. I bring the people what they have been looking for! Let's not waste another moment.'

The two men squabbled for several minutes more until most of those who had gathered had moved on. Without an audience, the argument soon petered out.

Thomas and Käthe hastily carried on along the

street.

'This is a very strange area of town,' she reported excitedly.

'This is the city I have grown used to,' Thomas replied.

The pair stopped and drank at several cafés, all of which brimmed with customers, crowds of gentlemen gesturing, bartering and brokering, creating a lively atmosphere. Finally, the pair found a place to settle. The lamps on the tables gleamed and the strange bohemian bar fell dark for a moment. It was a cosy den, with a low ceiling and intimate seating booths. As the room filled up, the air grew thick with cigarette smoke, rattling chatter and the clink of drinking glasses being toasted.

A merry satisfaction swept through Käthe as she soaked up the surroundings. To her, every individual was memorable. Not the parochial middle-classes that she was used to but a different trove of people altogether, artists and poets and probably some criminals too, all of them undoubtedly heroes of their own lives. Dressed up in pink and black and green, drinking rum and gin, reading each other's palms, smoking cigarettes from long holders, they were a claustrophobic menagerie of dark glamorous things with heavy eyes and sharp makeup. The men were thin and the women were full of angles, cheekbones and elbows. They had feathers in their hair and their dresses shimmered with a thousand sequins. People were cackling and debating. Rumour came around that a famous actor from the Babelsberg Studio was drinking there tonight. Käthe couldn't help but glance about for a chance sighting.

They sat in the corner of the bar, and for the first time all evening Thomas had Käthe all to himself. In the low yellow light from the lamp, he saw her up close, and the mayhem of the city was finally shut out.

From a distance, he found her striking to look at – she had a confident manner and a brave, modern sense of style. Up close, her youthful face and broad cheeks were beautiful in a different sort of way. Beneath her smile, her straight nose and large eyes, he saw an altogether more delicate expression, one that lingered so imperceptibly that he almost doubted his senses. The distraction of her high-fashion made this expression invisible from afar, but up close it was true and eloquent. He thought of her as full of character and of boundless energy. But now he could not miss the finesse of innocence she exuded, and that only endeared her to him all the more.

'I've always wondered what happens to people when they come to live in a big city like this. Do they become more open and outgoing because of all the stimulating sights and sounds? Does your appetite for living grow like that?' As Käthe spoke, she realised she was sharing some of her more eager thoughts. She noted to herself that she was completely at ease with Thomas and that her attraction to him was growing.

'I don't know what it feels like,' he said laughing. 'Perhaps I've been in Berlin for too long.'

They spoke for a while about his life in the city, and then she took her turn to describe the circumstances that had brought her to Potsdam. 'We have a large family, spread all over the country. I could probably find a relative to stay with in any city I chose.'

'Really? What about in Berlin?'

'My brother Arno moved here almost two years ago. But he never stays still for a moment. He likes the restlessness of it here.'

'Arno?' Thomas felt a sudden disturbance at hearing his name.

'He told me that corruption is around every corner

of Berlin. There are Communists plotting revolution –
perhaps even here in this bar. That kind of thing
intrigues him.'

Thomas listened. So far, he'd spent the evening in a
type of amnesia about the events on the roof terrace.
Now the memory of that night lit up again like curling
flames against the walls of his mind.

Mention of Arno also prompted a thought that had
long been nagging at the back of his mind: if it was Arno
who had approached him and Erich in the bar that night,
then why did he ask for a place to sleep? Why not go
straight to Käthe's apartment? Why go out begging when
he had a loving sister who lived in the same city? Käthe's
next statement seemed to supply the answer.

'Arno's trouble is that he gets himself into difficult
situations and then is too embarrassed to ask for help. It
just seems to happen to him. I think that's why he
disappears for months on end.'

'So he's unpredictable? Do you worry about him?'

'Sometimes. But I know he will appear one day. He
always turns up.'

Thomas sat back in his seat and hoped with all his
will that she was right. 'Where in Berlin does he live?' he
asked next as a new thought came to him.

'Arno? He lives in Hallesches Tor district, near the
U-Bahn station. He likes it there. I think it's all he can
afford.'

'He has an apartment there?'

'In a manner of speaking. He's actually living in a
roof attic above a bar, right in the pitch of the roof like
the head of the Holy Roman Empire!' she said grinning.

'What are you talking about?' Thomas asked.

'Oh, it's just a joke between me and my little brother.
And do you know what? He never takes his key with
him.'

'He leaves his place unlocked?'

'No, but he hides the key in an electricity box at the entrance. Frankly, that's really all you need to know about my brother!'

Käthe laughed to herself. 'And his glasses' – she started up again – 'remember we found them on the patio? Well, I worked out how they got there.'

'How?'

'My aunt must have left them. I will ask her next time I see her, but it had to be her. Arno probably made a visit to her, forgot his glasses, and then she left them at mine thinking I'd give them back to him. That's the only explanation I can think of.'

'I'd like to meet him one day,' Thomas said clumsily.

'Of course. You will soon, I'm sure. Now when are you going to answer my question?'

'What question?'

'What happened to you when you came to Berlin? Did it change you?'

'I don't remember.'

'Try harder then!' She gave him a playful shove.

'Nothing happened to me.'

'Nothing? But something must have happened. Didn't you feel inspired? Awoken?'

Thomas thought for a moment, feeling oddly agitated by the question. He was not satisfied with the discussion about Arno, and now he didn't want to move on from it. 'I thought about becoming an illegal gambler. And then a boxer, and then maybe a tattoo artist.'

'Now I know you're joking with me.'

'Berlin is beautiful and Berlin is ugly. It has everything else in between. The best way to explore it is on foot, especially at night. You should try it.'

'Is that so? But there are differences between men and women. Didn't you know that?' She arranged her

85

hands on her lap in a mock show of obedience. 'Well?'

'What do you mean?'

'Some people believe it's unseemly for a woman to be seen out on her own. They think she should wait for a man to take her. If you ask me, it's all a bit outdated.'

'You haven't seen much of the city then?'

'Not much. Now, there's an assignment for you. Won't you show me around?'

'Yes, of course.'

'Is it true that women dress up as men and men dress up as women? Where are these places? Can we go there tonight?'

'Where have you heard all these things?'

'In newspapers. In magazines. Haven't you seen these bizarre things that go on? What about tonight? Tonight has already been one of the oddest I've ever known.'

'It's not so strange once you see through the rumours. That's one of the triumphs of this place. It has managed to convince everyone else that only odd things happen here.'

'Is it all a myth then? Is it not true that some nightclubs have been closed down because the shows they put on are scandalous?' Käthe's eyes widened as she leaned forward and whispered, 'Is it a myth that artists and top-hatted businessmen and murderers all play cards around the same table?'

Thomas laughed.

'Criminals and saints! The sinners and the divine!' – Käthe was animated.

'The truth is, nobody really knows which stories are true and which are made up. But I know what I think.'

'Oh.' Käthe fell quiet. Thomas watched her eyes as they passed over the bar and the people gathered there. Then the gravest of thoughts passed through him, like an ill-wind passing through a house. Within an instant, he looked at her with the utmost dread as he tried to subdue images of her brother tumbling over the terrace railings.

He stood up and found himself telling her it was time to leave. He took her hand and led her out of the bar without giving any sort of explanation. She was confused for a moment, but then, under the mistaken impression that she was being led somewhere exciting, succumbed to the spontaneity without protest.

He led her across two streets in haste, and then when a tram rolled up beside them and he decided they would take it. Once seated, he was quiet and distracted. Käthe felt frazzled. The glasses of gin she'd drunk suddenly started to catch up with her, and she began to fall asleep, her head rocking and swaying towards Thomas' shoulder. They had not spoken a word since leaving the bar. The tram shuddered forwards in the direction of the Potsdamerplatz, grinding and rattling in all its parts. As Käthe turned her body around, yawning, she aligned her legs next to his and let her head tip onto his upper arm where it came to rest.

He felt her warm and moist breath rise to his face and he noticed threads of her hair clinging to the sleeve of his raincoat. The tram was all battered wood and corroded metal finishing. It felt cramped and cold that evening; a buzzing lamp overhead was enclosed in its casing, rattling like a fly inside a bottle.

For a moment Käthe half-woke and looked up. Her watery eyes were replete with contentment and tiredness. She put her head back on his arm and quickly fell asleep.

The firm weight of her head on his coat made him feel compelled to watch over her. Their lives had come together, and now, almost immediately, like planets and stars, they had begun to exert a force over one another. Their familiarity and closeness felt natural. How it had happened so quickly, he could hardly explain. Two weeks ago they were strangers, and now this! A cosmology was establishing, that was true. Attraction and momentum. Magnetism and intimacy. How remarkable life was!

For now, even though she was asleep, she reached over and took hold of his hand and clutched it, sinking her fingers into the gaps between his. He wanted to tell her how much he liked her, how much he enjoyed her probing questions, her optimism and excitement, and her energetic spirit. He wanted to hold her and keep her close and perhaps never let her go.

But what of Arno? Try as he might, Thomas was unable to push away the garish concern for the boy's fate. Was it really Käthe's brother who had fallen to his death from that great height? And what did she mean when she said he lived like the head of the Holy Roman Empire? Whatever she meant, more than ever, Thomas was filled with determination to disprove it was Arno, to find a different explanation.

THE DESCENT

"You are free and that is why you are lost" – Franz Kafka

13

The next morning, Thomas took a tram to Hallesches Tor, south of Mehringplatz. The tram moved over the hump of the bridge of the Landwehr Canal and came to a stop beside a war monument. He stepped off the tram and took in the panoramic view of the wide open space. It was lined with tall apartment blocks that were peppered with signs for hotels and cafés. A steady trickle of people passed over the canal bridge, men in hats, women in long coats, some people wheeling market-stall carts that were overburdened with furniture or books, teetering on the edge of collapse.

He walked beneath the awnings of numerous shops, grocers and hairdressers. He looked up at the buildings ahead of him, tall, austere stone blocks punctured by windows and heavy-set doors. Now he was here, he knew he was close to where Arno must live, nestled somewhere at the top of one of these blocks. If he could only locate the bar then he could hunt for the hidden key, gain access to the attic room and then perhaps find a hint of Arno's whereabouts.

He circled the streets several times over, searching through the cafés and hotels, not far from the U-Bahn station. Frustrated he went into a bar, ordered a Rüdesheimer coffee, and sat outside under the canopy. As he sipped, he glanced across the street at the other

91

cafés and bars and read the names in his head. And then he paused for a moment as he recollected and let the phrase *like the head of the Holy Roman Empire* sink through his mind. What did it mean? Was it a game that Käthe and Arno played as children? Perhaps he was supposed to be like Julius Caesar, the head of the Romans, the ruler, the emperor, the Kaiser. And then he saw it. Directly across the street, a place named Café Kaiser. Could it be the bar he'd been looking for, with the attic room sat in its pinnacle?

He quickly finished his coffee and crossed the road to a frosted glass door adjacent to the café. Through it he entered into a dingy hallway, with ceramic tiles and an elevator in the corner hung with a sign that read *Außer Betrieb* (Out of Order). He searched beneath the flight of stairs and found a narrow cupboard with a brass doorknob. When he opened it, he found a pile of cardboard boxes, a broom, a bucket, a dead rat and finally an electricity box. If what Käthe had said was true, then the key to Arno's apartment should be hidden in the electricity box somewhere.

He opened it and inside was a tangle of different coloured wires all laced together with clumps of brown spider web. Thomas ran his hand behind the lip of the wooden casing and located the jagged edge of a metal key. It had to be it. He took the key and quickly made his way up the staircase, assuming he had to climb as far as the steps would carry him to the attic. He climbed one floor after another until he reached the landing on the fifth floor. There didn't seem anywhere else to go to from this point. A tawdry-looking passageway led off in three directions, with wallpaper peeling off in great curls like a row of decrepit ancient scrolls.

At this moment, a woman emerged from one of the doorways. She was stern-looking, with square shoulders and a large, bra-less bosom. She was wearing nothing but a white undergarment and long brown stockings pulled up to her thighs. One of the shoulder straps had slipped down her arm, revealing a narrow tan line over her shoulder.

Thomas asked if she knew anyone by the name of Arno Hiller. The woman took a moment to consider the question. Her eyes shifted to one side in deepest thought. Then she pointed along the corridor and up to a hatch in the ceiling. Here was an extra flight of steps in the form of a wooden ladder fastened to the wall.

'Have you seen him recently?' Thomas asked.

'Who? That boy? He comes and goes every once in a while. Can't say I've seen him in the past few days mind you. I am not his mother, of course, so how would I know when he was last here?'

Thomas told her a made-up story of how he was an old friend of Arno's and that he'd come to surprise him. It was a piece of information the woman seemed wholly indifferent to. She pulled the shoulder strap back up her arm and disappeared into her own apartment.

Thomas took himself up the steep ladder and, using the key he'd found, tried the padlock that sealed the hatch – the padlock sprung open.

Inside the attic, he found a rather despairing set of circumstances. He entered a narrow space cut across at angles by the triangular pitch of the roof. There was a bicycle with a flat tyre, a washing line with a pair of socks pegged to it, a single chair with a sunken rattan seat, and in the far corner, a crowd of empty beer bottles. It was desperately bare inside. He could see the underside of the roof tiles that covered the building, and even the grey globs of cement that bound the tiles together. It was like he was in the very outer shell of the building.

He went searching for clues, something that might

tell him more about Arno's life here. There was very little to go on. The room had no carpet nor any rugs. There were no curtains over the windows either, and instead of a wardrobe or a chest of drawers, there was a plywood tea crate with a jumble of clothes tossed in.

Thomas rummaged through these garments but found nothing. He examined the bicycle and peered over the collection of empty beer bottles, then went to one of the windows and opened it to reveal an impressive view over Hallesches Tor.

Then he heard a voice call up to him. It was the woman from the floor below. Her face was peering up through the hatch, her hands planted on her hips.

'Everything alright up there?' she called out. 'My daughter says he hasn't been to his room for at least two weeks now.'

'Two weeks?'

'I asked her. That's what she says.'

Thomas went over to the bed that sat at one end of the attic and turned over the sheets and pillow, still hoping to find something of significance. Then he noticed something. On top of a bedside shelf was a slip of paper. It had been ripped in two and only one half remained. It had nothing on it except for two words: 'Midnight. Clär...' – with a torn edge cutting through the second word. He scoured the floor for the other half, checking behind and under the bed. He searched the rest of the room but the other half was no where to be found. He returned his attention to the slip in his hand. The word 'Midnight' was underlined in pencil. The other word was less easy to decipher. What was it? Could it be a name – the name of a person, even the name of another city? Even with just the first four letters, Thomas felt sure he'd seen it before.

He took the paper and folded it into his pocket. He

was aware of staying too long; and having already been seen by the neighbour downstairs, he realised he must be careful. If news of Arno's disappearance reached the police, there was a chance he might be implicated. He left the attic and on his way out, returned the key to the electricity box just as he'd found it.

Outside, dusk was just arriving and the streetlamps above were beginning to flicker into life. The streets were busy with comings and goings, commuters catching trams or rushing into a nearby U-Bahn station. Above, flashing advertisements floated and hung, all the way up to the rooftops. The broad avenues stretched out in front of him, lined with their enormous grey-brown buildings made from blocks of stone as big as automobiles. Thomas went past the beer halls with their dependable middle-class patrons, and heard the usual whisper of the prostitutes nestled in doorways, 'Want a date, lovely?'

He boarded a tram back to Potsdamerplatz and dropped into a local *kneipe*, one of those dark beer cellars where everyone stood up to drink. He ordered a beer and ate a boiled egg from the pickle jar. It was just as he was thinking about the torn slip of paper he'd found in Arno's attic room when he felt the strangest sensation come over him. For he had the distinct feeling that he was being watched.

From the corner of his eye, he glanced to the opposite end of the bar and saw a tall man in a bowler hat seemingly reading a newspaper. There was something familiar about him – Thomas thought he'd seen him on the tram a few minutes before.

He had to test out his instinct, so he swallowed the last of his pickled egg, took the greasy steps back up to street level and turned towards the Kurfürstendamm. He could see a flower stall just up ahead, with red and white flares of rose and lily bouquets. He stopped at the flower stall and glanced over his shoulder: twenty yards behind, the man in the bowler hat was just emerging from the beer cellar steps.

Thomas moved on. There was a tiny establishment further down that belonged to a Jewish family who sold lavish boxes of chocolate with ribbons tied around them. It usually stayed open until late in order to catch the office workers on their way home. When he arrived he found the shop had a smashed window and was boarded up with planks of wood. Someone had scrawled the words 'Jew here' in large, ugly letters.

He paused at the boarded up shop and pretended to peer inside between the planks of wood. Looking to his side, he noticed the man in the bowler hat had also stopped, still close behind. Thomas then turned onto a side road where a café with outdoor seating had sprawled across the pavement. He wove between the chairs and tables and out to the other side. A minute later, he checked behind him and saw the same man in the bowler hat passing through the same café seating.

There could be no doubt he was being followed. Had he been seen entering into Arno's attic? Was it a policeman in pursuit? Or some unknown rogue accomplice?

Thomas found his way back onto the Kurfürstendamm and stopped again, this time looking into the window of an apartment store. The twinkling lights of the window display allowed him to see his own image in the window. He waited now, staring at the reflection, examining the street behind him in the glass. After a few moments he saw the man in the bowler hat pass behind. As he went by, the gentleman looked at Thomas with a hard stare in the mirrored glass. He didn't stop but kept on walking along the street, finally crossing the road and disappearing into the night. It was there and then that Thomas realised that if he continued his search for the truth about Arno, then he would have to keep his sharpest wits about him.

14

The next day, Thomas travelled south, past Tempelhof airport and onto Berlin's Mariendorf district. He was going to visit Käthe's uncle. Konrad Hiller was a war veteran; when he answered his door, he used a stick and walked with a pronounced limp.

'Pleased to meet you,' Thomas said, greeting him politely.

'So you're the boy that Käthe has been talking about?' Herr Hiller passed his fingers over a large blond moustache that tickled the underside of his top lip.

On the surface, Thomas was there to buy a second-hand motorcycle from the old soldier. He also came with an ulterior motive: to glean more information about Arno. It had been exactly three weeks since the incident on the roof terrace, and Thomas was beginning to find fresh moments of purpose. Learning more about Arno was an impulse he had to act on.

The motorbike was another. He pictured himself sat astride the engine, rumbling through the streets of Berlin like a drum-roll. He had begun to crave new freedoms. He imagined Käthe's clinging on in all her liveliness, speeding bravely up the Kurfürstendamm and out of Berlin, without pause or consideration for anything but themselves.

'Come on in from that wet,' Herr Hiller said. He

guided Thomas beneath his raised arm as drops of rain began to fall. A proud looking gentleman, Herr Hiller was dressed in a woollen suit and a necktie. He had combed blond hair that blended almost imperceptibly with his fair skin.

'I'm told you are selling all of your possessions,' Thomas said, recalling the explanation Käthe had given him about why the motorbike was for sale.

'Yes, it's true.'

'Why is that? I'm interested.'

'I am returning to nature. I'm taking leave of all man-made goods.' Herr Hiller gave a deliberately civilised smile to convince his visitor that he was serious. 'I have been considering it for some time now. Everything I own, I'm selling. I believe it will make all the difference for me.'

Thomas thought about his choice. Giving up on life's pleasures seemed like an impossible concept. Still, he liked the soldier, who had something immemorial in his bearing. It was as if he belonged to a different epoch of time to everyone else.

'Well, I have always wanted to own a motorcycle,' the visitor eventually said, 'so we can do each other a favour.'

'You like engines?'

'I want to be able to travel at speed. Bicycles are tedious.'

'Ah yes, speed. Speed is useful, to be sure. But patience offers us something that speed cannot.' At this, the man hobbled on his crutch into an adjacent room and came back carrying a book. Eagerly he opened the pages. 'This is my guide,' he said, '*The Decay of the Modern World*. One of its messages is that speed is a symptom of a disturbed mind.'

Thomas nodded as he listened.

'In the author's opinion,' Herr Hiller went on, 'this age of machines is bringing about the demise of our basic civilisation. Over the next hundred years, the collapse of our society will take place and we will become slaves to automation. We will not run them; they will run us. We have seen hints in the past few years, but worse is to come. Much worse. The answer? To embrace nature. I'm going to re-discover the German empathy for nature. I intend to reconnect with it, and the first thing I must do is rid myself of all factory-made objects. It's a way of purifying the whole inner system.'

The man's hands were large and thick-set, and they moved through the pages of the book with an excited cadence, like a pair of overweight legs dancing. 'Here, take a look.'

Thomas took the book and thumbed through a few of the densely typed pages. Beside him, the invalid soldier peered on, his smile still fixed in place, patiently awaiting an opinion from his guest. Thomas thought he seemed remarkably optimistic for someone predicting the fall of civilisation.

'So your solution is to leave everything behind?' Thomas said.

'No, my solution is to live life to the full! That is nature's way. Have you ever watched a wild animal move through its territory? It is completely immersed in what it's doing. That's nature's way.'

'Well, that sounds very true.' Thomas said, warming to the idea.

'Most people don't seem to remember this anymore,' Herr Hiller continued. 'There's too much interest in human affairs. Politics. Money. Business. There is fighting on the streets everyday. They have forgotten about what lies beneath. I ask you: have you ever seen our country in such a mess?'

100

'What do you mean?'

'Well, only recently a boy was killed. Not very old, they say. Thrown from the roof of a building. Here in Berlin! It is shocking to hear such things. All for the sake of politics.'

Thomas stopped, his senses suddenly quickened. 'A boy? Thrown from a building?' Panic rose into his throat. 'Where did you hear that?'

Herr Hiller took a pile of papers from a nearby table and found the item he was referring to. He passed the sheet to Thomas, who read the words silently to himself. *Boy thrown from rooftop. Communist conspiracy to protect the guilty.* The words were printed in large text, an attention-grabbing headline on a single-sheet pamphlet.

'I don't understand,' Thomas said. 'Where is this from?'

'It was given to me in the street.'

'Do you think it's true?'

'It's all politics. Truth doesn't come into it. They're just looking for the spark that will light the bonfire. A child gets killed. That's just the sort of thing that can set off an explosion.'

'Are you saying that Communists killed this boy as a provocation?'

Hiller responded cryptically, to Thomas' frustration. 'I'm saying violence serves agendas.'

Thomas looked at the pamphlet again. *Communist conspiracy to protect the guilty* – what could it possibly mean? Erich was no Communist. In fact, as far as Thomas knew, Erich's sympathies were in the other direction entirely. He believed in the unity of his nation. He thought Germany should be self-sufficient, and he believed communism was a threat to that.

'Tell me about the boy,' Thomas said. 'Where did it happen?'

'In the suburbs most likely. That's where sentiment is at its most unsteady.'

Thomas shook his head in disbelief. Could it really be the same story, the same boy he saw tumble over the side of the terrace in Potsdam? If it was, then the news was out there, circulating in pamphlets like this. Had a body been found? If so, then who had found it and why hadn't it reached the newspapers?

'Well, I don't believe in rumours,' Thomas eventually said.

'Rumours have a way of turning into facts,' Herr Hiller replied.

'Can I ask you something else?' Thomas said, 'Have you seen your nephew recently?'

'Who do you mean?'

'Arno, Käthe's brother.'

'Arno? Oh no, not in months. He's away in a world of his own.'

'In what way?'

'Women. Drink. Whatever young men get up to these days.'

'So you haven't heard anything from him?'

'No. Why? Should I have done?' Herr Hiller began combing his yellow moustache with his fingernails.

'Käthe has been waiting for him to visit her, that's all.'

'She'll be waiting for months.' The old soldier broke into a smile, as if a part of him admired the sort of life he imagined Arno to be living.

Thomas felt a raised sense of uncertainty as he considered the possibility that news of what Erich had done had begun to circulate. Facts and rumours were converging upon a single truth. But as yet, to his frustration, he couldn't confirm what that truth was.

Then, with a strange compulsion, he desperately

wanted to be astride the motorbike, to feel the hum of the engine beneath his body, riding through the city, free and fierce and alone.

'Please, can you show me the bike now?'

The veteran agreed and the two men went from the house to a small warehouse at the rear. The rain had stopped and the clouds were beginning to break open. The old soldier went in, and a few minutes later Thomas heard the chug and growl of a petrol engine that roused in him a fresh enlivenment. The noise grew louder, then it went softer for a moment and began to purr. Eventually the sound revealed itself in the shape of a fine black motorcycle, ridden for one last time by its current owner.

Steering a wide U-shaped path, Herr Hiller repeatedly passed the front of the warehouse before finally stopping the motorcycle next to Thomas. The rider climbed off the bike and lowered the stand to keep it upright. Standing back, he admired the machine with his knuckles resting on his hips and a layer of sweat greasing his face. The engine gurgled for a few more seconds, then went quiet, leaving just the ticking of cooling metal.

It was a handsome item. The black frame was covered in dents, lending the bike an aged character. The silver engine was squeezed beneath a tanned leather saddle. Two canvas pannier bags were fixed on a rack above the rear wheel. Every joint, piston and sprocket glowed with lubricant.

'What do you think?' the old man asked.

'I think it's wonderful.'

'Four-stroke v-twin. Three-speed gearbox. I once rode through the mountains of Bavaria on this machine.'

'Sounds great.'

The two men spoke for a short while longer before

an exchange of cash was made.

Finally, Thomas climbed aboard his new vehicle. He rammed the pedal with his foot, starting the engine first time, and squeezed the handle to pull away. This was it, he thought. His new eight-hundred-cc bike, with a top speed of who-knew-what. He could cover so much more ground on it, beyond Berlin, wherever he wanted to go. Everyone would hear him coming now, rumbling through the vertical stone valleys of the city for miles around.

He said goodbye to Konrad Hiller, choked the rubber bulb of the horn to make it honk, then rode the bike back to his district of Berlin. He went by his apartment, along the Lietzenburgerstrasse, the Schillstrasse, the Schönenberger Ufer, not slowing for obstacles or other traffic. What a wonderful feeling it was, to be free and dynamic like this.

Then it came to him: the shift in his heart he was truly after. With the bike between his knees, neither Berlin or Erich could intimidate him.

Over the course of the next few days, he rode his motorbike whenever possible and quickly achieved a degree of mastery over it. His journeys left no doubt in his mind that he was now something of a spectacle, a dazzling sight, a noise and a force for the inert sensibilities of the masses to reckon with. The city would know him; his passions would turn Berlin from a garish gothic metropolis into a glistening palace.

And after every ride he would go to his room and fall onto his bed in submission to a deep and satisfying fatigue. And when he fell asleep, he did so with perfect ease, entering into tranquil and mysterious dreams that one might take as evidence of a newly awoken mind.

15

During the week, a policeman had been killed at a workers' rally. He'd been kicked to death after intervening in a fight between Nazi and Communist demonstrators. The *Berliner Tageblatt* covered the story in detail, offering a series of fiercely targeted editorials designed to galvanise the opinion-holding classes. Out on the streets, there were more pamphleteers and speech-makers than Thomas could ever remember.

He rode on his motorbike towards Berlin Cathedral. The pamphlets that Konrad Hiller had shared prompted him to seek out the Communist rally that Malik had spoken about previously. He couldn't ignore the rumours and the coincidence of a boy having been thrown from a rooftop.

He saw crowds up ahead. There was chanting and singing. As he approached, he noticed that many of them were carrying placards and waving flags.

Then, amongst their faces, he picked out the prominent jawline of young Malik.

'What a fine day!' the youngster called out when he saw Thomas.

'Where have you been?' Thomas shouted back, gesturing for his roommate to come over. He'd not seen Malik for the last five days.

'Staying with friends,' Malik replied as he stepped

away from the march. He was holding a sign that read
'*Die Juden sind unser Unglück*', ('The Jews are our
misfortune') which he handed over to a fellow protester
to carry. 'Wonderful that you could make it,' he said, his
familiar smile widening. 'Now let's walk and you can tell
me if you are still in love with that girl. What was her
name? Luise? No that's not it.'

'Käthe,' Thomas said, amused by Malik's turn of
phrase about love.

'Of course.'

'Why have you not been staying at the apartment?'
Thomas asked. 'I haven't seen you in days.'

Malik explained he'd been working night-shifts at a
warehouse in order to pay off some urgent debts.
'Hardest work I've ever done in my life, but I can't
complain about the money,' he said.

As they walked, Thomas began to notice certain
things about Malik's appearance. He saw that one of his
shoes was badly split along the outside edge and was
almost falling off his foot. And on his right hand he had
a long scar running from his thumb across his palm that
was clearly fresh. Then he noticed the first few fingers of
his left hand were stained with tobacco, and after that, he
found his aroma to be quite repulsive – not just a strong
smell of cigarettes, but a whole zoo of disgusting smells
wafting from him. Thomas tried not to react to any of
these things, but he couldn't help ascribe their cause to a
downturn in the boy's fortunes.

'I'm here for the rally,' Thomas said. 'Are you still
with the Communists?'

'Those rotten Communists! No way! They wouldn't
take me as a member. They said I was a petty-bourgeois
worm. Me! No backbone they said! If they could see me
at the warehouse, they'd think again. The truth is, they
were frightened of me because I am an intellectual and I

represent what they cannot be: I make the best of what I've got. Call me disloyal if you want, but I say that *they* have no backbone. Anyway, they are all philistines. All talk. A fad.'

'So you have new affiliations?'

'I have made some new connections, yes. These people care only about our country and our people. It's a better vision of the future.' Malik grabbed Thomas' arm. 'Come with us. We intend to hijack the rally. We're marching *against* the Communists today.'

Thomas looked around. He saw legions of men all trudging in the same direction. Some carried banners; others carried pitchforks.

'All the men from my warehouse are going to be there,' Malik went on. 'And they say that hundreds of farmers are coming into the city to join in. It's going to be quite an event. Solidarity is everything these days.'

'It sounds dangerous.'

Malik grinned. 'I hope so.'

Thomas agreed to go. After a few minutes walk, they came upon a street busy with even more people. Malik grew exhilarated when he saw the crowd, though he found it hard to explain what was really happening. He moved through at a pace, not in the least concerned by his disintegrating shoe or his injured hand – except to give it a quick brush against his leg to wipe away any blood. All the time he kept saying, 'Soon it will happen. Any minute now.'

Beneath the spring sun, a group of men dressed in white shirts paced down the street, parting the crowds and bawling '*Deutschland, erwache!*' (Wake up, Germany!). Lacking the necessary discipline, they failed to keep a military-style formation, though not for the want of trying.

Thomas heard mention of Poles and Slavs and Jews.

107

'Destroy the alien forces!' one man shouted into his ear.

Malik led the way towards what seemed to be the heart of the occasion. Men of all ages, from all backgrounds, soldiers, builders, farmers and students, pushed past each other, all of them high-spirited or highly-strung, with a combination of fervour and agitation, all of them casting their eyes left and right in search of a direction to move in or rally behind.

'We're protesting about everything,' Malik said. 'Versailles. The internal Jewish threat. The greater German destiny to expand eastward.'

'Destiny?'

'We need more living space for crops and cattle. And we need to overcome the decaying races before they choke us.'

Further along the street, a smaller but more intense gathering had formed. It concentrated on a single figure, a man stood on top of a cart who was vocalising an unscripted speech. He was shouting and waving his arms. Around him a couple of other men held boards, one of which had written on the letters NSDAP and the other a slogan which read *Germany Unite!*

'Nazis,' Thomas surmised.

'These are true German socialists,' Malik replied. 'No lousy Russians here. They believe in the true German worker. They believe in the value of honesty, the union of men and the struggle against the animals.'

Thomas looked about him. It was the city he knew, yet all these faces, full of zeal and antagonism, cast it in a different light.

The speech-maker expressed himself with great gusto. He was a small man with a slight lisp, but his words carried an impressive distance. 'We are a working nation, and we demand the right to work. Germany awake! Berliners! It's time to rise up!'

Malik turned to Thomas and grinned. 'We have arrived at just the right time,' he said.

The speaker went on: 'The destiny of this nation is in jeopardy. Jews loom over us, but we will not be bribed. The Bolsheviks threaten us, but they will not devour us. The great lie they have brought on the people of Russia is an affront to their true nationhood. I shall remind you of a simple truth. You have nothing but your country! The death of your nation is your own death!'

As he spoke, he thrust out his arm and began picking out members of the crowd with a pointed finger. 'Your death! And your death! And your death! The next truth is simple too. No victory over degradation is possible without the unity of the people, and for this noble cause we must overcome fear. Seek out your nation, then you will understand your part in the whole. This victory is worth fighting for and we must all stand up and be counted as one.'

All through his speech, the man was singling out audience members by pointing at individuals. Malik had begun to push to the front, wanting the speaker's finger to land on him too. Thomas began to follow, but the concentration of the crowd was too great to get through. Evidently, the orator had animated the whole hoard of men, who began to push forward all together. At the same time, people were arriving from behind, exerting more pressure, sending rippled surges through the crowd. His rousing words led everyone to cheer and agree with him, and for the air to swell with an atmosphere of revolution.

Setting the messages of hate aside, Thomas found the idea of a greater Germany energising. Every individual in harmony with the whole – what a powerful force for a resurgent nation.

Evidently, he had lost track of Malik. He was sorry to

lose him but was glad to have seen the young student; in fact, reluctant though he might be to admit it, he was envious of the boy's limitless enthusiasm.

(Thomas later heard that a street brawl had broken out between the Communist demonstrators and the Nazi crowds who came to disrupt them. Men swung fists at each other, sometimes pinning their opponents against a wall for others to pummel. They wrestled on the floor with legs flailing while others leered above laying the boot in. Some stripped away their shirts and were seen dashing down the street half-naked toward the next concentration of violence. Moments of calm and negotiation were quickly lost when someone uttered the wrong word. There were punches in faces, broken noses, ears torn, eyes gouged. Fighters took off their belts and began whipping their opponents or hauling them along the street with the belts hooked under the chin. Chairs were thrown, nearby bars looted for glass bottles and anything else that could be used as a weapon. Those with pitchforks swung them and thrust them like bayonets. One man was stabbed through the thigh. The most remarkable thing was that no one was killed.)

After the rally, Thomas returned home still reeling from the event. As he approached his building, he found Herr Beenken outside, scrubbing the street floor with a broom and bucket. Thomas attempted to hurry past, offering a feigned smile but Beenken would not let him go so easily.

'Thomas,' he whined. 'You're back!'

'Yes, I'm back.' Thomas turned and passed a glance to the old landlord.

'It's been busy here,' Beenken said, his eyes flickering. 'Would you like to know what has happened?'

'I don't have the time right now.'

'You have two options,' Beenken interrupted with force. 'The first is to listen to me, the second is to pack your bags.'

'Yes, fine,' Thomas fired back. 'What is it?'

It was obvious Beenken was in a state of distress. His hands were trembling, clinging to the broom like two barnacled lobster claws. His eyes were watery and his face was anointed with perspiration.

'This mess for one.' Beenken gestured to the ground. He was scrubbing away the remnants of a swastika sign that had been daubed on the street in black paint. 'Someone did this. I've been cleaning it up for two hours now.'

'You're nearly there,' Thomas replied, half expecting to be recruited into the clean-up operation. The swastika was large, about two-metres square. Thomas had seen plenty of those at the rally. 'You're doing a great job!' Thomas exclaimed, trying to move away.

'Keep your voice down! I'm afraid we're being listened to.'

'By who?'

'That bastard upstairs!'

'Who?'

'The one who threatened to punch me earlier. I know it's sensible to have other business interests, but this? I don't know…'

'Who are you talking about?'

'The tenant on the top floor.' Beenken paused. 'He's here to cause trouble. Money. That's his rotten business. It's always about money.'

Thomas didn't respond. He didn't understand and he didn't want to.

'Will you come with me upstairs?' Beenken turned firm again. 'I will not allow violence in my building. I cannot stand by and watch.' Then he paused for a

111

moment. When he pushed his hair across his brow, Thomas could see his hand was shaking. Muffled shouts came echoing down the stairwell and out into the street. 'Will you go first?' Beenken pleaded.

'Fine,' Thomas said. 'Move out of my way.' He began to climb the stairs with Beenken behind muttering to himself.

'Gambling, I won't have it. Not in my building.'

'What's going on up there?'

'He's set up a club in his room. They play cards and bet on them. At all hours. And they fight.'

As they approached the next floor the shouts grew cruder and more alarming. Yet, just as they were reaching the top of the staircase, the voices all of a sudden fell quiet.

Just then, the lock in the door began to turn. A second later, the door swung open and a man came bursting out onto the landing. Thomas immediately took several steps backwards and almost knocked Beenken down the stairs behind him. The pair teetered on the same step for a moment, treading on each other's feet, until finally they found their balance and were able to take stock of the man who looked down at them from the landing above.

The figure had an improbable air of comedy. He was wearing a suit, one that was so loose-fitting it obviously didn't belong to him. His build was slight and there was an edgy confidence about him that was hard to trust. He tottered left and right on a pair of short legs beneath a disproportionately long torso. His face wore a petulant sort of grin, which spoke of aggression and bemusement at the same time. A closely-trimmed beard caused his face to appear fatter than perhaps it was, accentuating a pair of sunken eyes and rubbery cheeks. Stopped in his tracks he passed his eyes over Thomas, all the time keeping his wry smirk intact. When he saw Beenken, his eyes widened and he seemed to relax a little.

Thomas returned the gesture by scanning the man from top to toe. Just then, a woman appeared behind him. She bounded out with great energy and momentum, animated by a purpose that was difficult to pinpoint. Her form was plump, her silhouette circular. Her face too was round, made pale and flat by white makeup. Thomas caught her gaze. She smiled, or scowled, it was hard to tell which. She glanced at the other man, and then upon seeing Beenken, she began to make an exasperated scream.

Beenken raised himself up to the landing and went to pacify the woman. He crept up to her with his arms outstretched and a pathetic expression on his face, something of a paternal smile; something too of a simpering grin. As he reached the woman, the other man stepped between them and a minor squabble broke out.

From what Thomas could make out, amid the raised arms and voices, the woman was accused of pocketing too much of the gambling takings and was now due to suffer for it. What surprised Thomas was Beenken's role, for he clearly knew more about the situation than he had first let on. It seemed as soon as the squat man raised his objection, Beenken immediately changed sides and started demanding money too, at first copying the phrases of the other man parrot-fashion, and then proposing his own arguments.

'Now now,' Beenken was saying to the woman. 'If you take the money, you must give it back. It's only fair.'

Thomas found Beenken's duplicity wholly distasteful.

'You must understand that everyone needs to make a living,' Beenken went on. 'Please, do as he says.'

Eventually, the fracas died down but not before the aggrieved woman had charged everyone present with conspiracy, including Thomas, whom she couldn't trust because he was 'too quiet.' By this point, Beenken had colluded so much with the other man that he convinced himself that he too was owed money, and moreover, he appeared to be quite enjoying himself. He stood with his hands holding his hips, his big unhealthy face smiling happily. A moment later he pulled out his pipe and began to pack it with tobacco, chuckling to himself.

In a show of disgust, the woman paced back into the bedroom and slammed the door shut. At this, Beenken and the other man began to laugh, patting each other on the shoulders to prove their victory. Thomas looked on unimpressed. He stood now halfway down the stairs and began to make a retreat. The two men on the landing were too consumed with each other to notice, joking and agreeing that the money they came for could wait for another day. They looked the best of friends as they talked about the joys of smoking and where Beenken purchased his tobacco. Thomas scowled at the unlikely cohorts as he returned to his room. Truly, foul-play had taken place.

16

No matter where Thomas looked, Erich had completely disappeared from sight. Thomas couldn't find him, so he decided he would visit Ingrid Koerner – Erich's lover. The couple had been engaged for twelve months. Like Erich, she came from a wealthy family, and like him, possessed a self-confident, theatrical side. She smoked cigarettes through an ivory holder and had a taste for whiskey. She also paraded herself as a libertine, an attitude which lent her an avant-garde style. It was almost as if she thought herself to be famous; the flip-side to this was a private self-consciousness where she couldn't act without thinking of the effect on her appearance. Thomas once saw her undress through an open doorway, an image which he was sure she had orchestrated deliberately.

He arrived at her apartment at exactly noon. In stark contrast to her carefully tuned appearance, Ingrid's apartment was a cluttered trove. In the entrance hall three clarinets were lined up along the wall, none of which she could play. Rose petals lay in numerous shallow dishes. A hat stand stood in the corner blossomed with brightly coloured bonnets. A stack of framed Dürer prints was piled up against a table ready to be hung. In the main living room, there was an original oil painting by Jana Constein – Ingrid had always fancied

115

herself as something of a patron and promised to buy more work from the artist. Below the picture, a pile of typed manuscripts – a novel she was working on – were strewn haphazardly across a desk. A miniature of Michelangelo's David stood nearby, strung with brightly-coloured bead-necklaces. A single shelf in the middle of the wall stored a volume of encyclopaedias, and on the rug below, a stack of foreign literature translated into German. This charming mess was her way of keeping her world from drying up. But anyone who spent some time with Ingrid would inevitably sense that it was also a burden to her, since those unread books and those incense sticks not yet burnt were signs of a restless, dissatisfied spirit.

She had a perfectly oval face, symmetrical in every part, shallow blue eyes that were simple in an elegant way, and a slender nose bearing on a mouth that was neatly pursed. Thomas felt her recent bouts of despondency were perversions of a truer, more colourful character. It did not suit her to be so solemn.

As soon as he arrived, she told him they were leaving. 'Erich is not here,' she said. 'It's just the two of us today.'

'Where is he?' Thomas asked. 'I've been looking for him all over the city.'

'He might be with us later. That's if he remembers. He's been impossible recently. For now you'll have to put up with just me.'

Thomas had brought some toffees and fudges in a brown bag, which he opened and offered to Ingrid. She laughed with condescension as if sweets were an affront to her higher tastes, but took a handful anyway.

They travelled on foot to Ingrid's parent's house that was just three streets away. Thomas had been there before; he'd eaten and drunk wine in their little pavilion

116

at the bottom of the huge garden, and played badminton and other games on the lawn behind the trees.

They bypassed the main entrance of the house and went straight into the garden and to the pavilion adorned with wisteria in flower. Ingrid immediately took a seat on the steps with her head in the shade and her legs in the sun as she liked to do. They sat quietly for a time in the warm rays of light.

'I am relaxed here in the sun,' she said. 'I hate that apartment. It's so dark.'

'You are luckier than you realise,' Thomas replied, sounding envious.

Ingrid changed the subject. 'Have you sat for the next phase of Jana's painting? She really is a marvel at her artistry.'

'I've not been called yet but I'm interested to see how she captures us all.'

'It's a very odd thing to have someone study you for two hours. It's quite disturbing to tell the truth. Take my advice. If you concentrate on your breathing you'll find it much easier to stay still. When we were on the roof terrace, I didn't move a muscle the entire time.'

Thomas paused on the thought, trying to hold back the inevitable disconcerted feeling that the topic produced.

'How is Käthe?' she asked as if reading his deepest thoughts.

'She's good. I took her out last week.'

'Wonderful. She seems like a nice girl.'

'She has many good attributes,' Thomas said rather formally, failing to suppress a smile.

'You like her then?' Ingrid said teasingly.

'So my instincts tell me, yes.'

'I'm happy to hear it.'

'I'm glad you are, now can we change the subject

please?'

'To what?'

'First of all, you can tell me where Erich is. You never did say.'

'I don't know where he is. I never know. You might say that's one of his charms. Actually, we're not speaking much at the moment.'

'Not speaking? Have you had an argument?'

'I wouldn't say that. He's just drunk most of the time, so I do my best to avoid him. He goes through these phases. He's idealistic and stubborn. That's a terrible combination, because he thinks he knows better than anyone else.'

Thomas looked across the lawn at the large house perched on the shelf of green, as he wondered what lay behind Erich's behaviour.

'He has no structure in his life!' Ingrid started up again, this time with more agitation. 'Nothing! And he's been arguing with his parents. They want him to go abroad, perhaps for a job with an embassy. Can you imagine him? I walked in on an argument between them just a few days ago. It wasn't nice. They are concerned for him.'

'Do you think he will go?'

'No, it could never happen.'

Thomas considered. 'I don't know. He's wayward, but he's not incapable.'

'In this case, I think he is. He cannot stand politicians – he thinks they are all Communists and backstabbers. Can you imagine his father's reaction if he heard that?' Ingrid continued: 'And there's his brother too, of course.'

Erich's older brother, Johann, had been killed in the war. It was a cruel shock for a family that thought it was indestructible.

'What about his brother?' Thomas asked.

Ingrid turned towards Thomas. In her eyes, he spotted a cruel excitement as if she relished an opportunity to betray Erich's confidence. 'They were very close. Johann taught Erich everything. He's still very bitter about his death. In fact, I don't think he's ever got over it.'

'Do you know what actually happened to Johann?'

'I don't think anybody knows but there was some hushed talk of him being a spy. That's why Erich himself never fought. He's the right age, you know? He could have enlisted, but the family made sure he stayed at home. He became a sort of jewel to his parents after Johann died. That's why they are so generous to him – and so worried.'

'I can understand that,' Thomas said, thinking of his own experiences of the war. He had an undistinguished military career, stationed just about as far from action as anybody could be, with an aircraft maintenance company in Oberschleissheim where he spent three years executing pointless marching drills and restoring aircraft camouflage.

'It was Johann's birthday last week. I expect Erich went to visit the cemetery.'

'He doesn't speak about his brother very much, does he?'

'Hardly ever. These days he's not very reflective. He prefers to live in the moment, as you know.'

'I do,' Thomas agreed, nodding.

Ingrid smiled. 'Don't mention anything to him, will you? That we were talking about him.'

'If I ever find him, I won't mention a thing.'

After a while, Ingrid stood up from the step and walked barefooted across the lawn, heading towards the base of a tree where a number of hand-sized rocks had been left. She picked up one of the rocks and carried it onto the lawn where she carefully set it down in the middle of the grass.

'Let's not talk about Erich anymore,' she said. She went back to the base of the tree and took another rock. Then she said. 'Listen.'

'Listen?'

'Shhhhsss! Just listen.'

Thomas fell quiet. A few moments passed, birdsong came down from the trees and the rustle of a nearby stream could be heard. Then another noise joined in. It was a melody of clocks chiming faintly from inside the house. It was three o'clock.

'Can you hear them?' she said.

'The clocks? Yes, I can. How many clocks are here?'

'Dozens.' Ingrid went off around the side of the pavilion.

'What are you doing?'

A moment later she came back with another rock. 'This one is for later. I'm making a clock,' she said.

Thomas noticed the position of the first rock on the lawn. It was placed exactly where the pitch of the gazebo roof was casting its shadow. The shape of the roof meant the shadow was like a huge arrow pointing across the grass toward the house.

'You're making a sundial!' Thomas shouted out happily.

'Yes! I make them all the time. Come over here,' she called.

Thomas got to his feet and hurried after her as she went into the woods. After following for a short time, they came upon a clearing of long grass in the middle of the wood. There were small piles of rocks set out in a steadily curving arc with a gap of about ten feet between them; it was obvious now what they were for.

'I used the shadow of the tall poplar tree over there,' Ingrid said as she pointed toward the sun. The shadow of the tree fell across the open space, crossing over the line of rock piles.

'Every hour I come back and add another pile. I like watching the shadows move and change. Of course, they're only accurate for one day of the year. Tomorrow, the sun will have shifted by a few degrees.'

'Are there any more?'

'Lots.'

They walked through the wooded area and out where the path came up beside the house. Along the way she showed him the place where she'd made a sundial the previous autumn using leaves arranged in heaps. Then she showed him a tiny dial she'd made on a brick wall using the shadow cast by a twig forced into the mortar. In all, there were at least a dozen sundials dotted randomly about, and the remnants of half-a-dozen more. She said, 'Most of them don't last very long – the gardener moves them if the wind doesn't. That's fine though. Change is a part of the idea.'

At that moment the clocks chimed, which alerted Thomas to a new thought. He was reminded that the bells of Potsdam were striking six o'clock at the very moment he saw Erich grappling with the boy on the roof terrace. For the first time, he wondered if the time mattered.

It was only as the chimes stopped that he looked up and saw Erich striding across the lawn towards them.

'Can anyone tell me the time?' Erich joked, recognising what they were up to. He walked into the shadow of the pavilion and kissed Ingrid on the cheek.

'Hello Thomas. Are you well?'

'We missed you this afternoon,' Thomas replied after he realised his hunt for Erich was over. 'Ingrid has been

121

showing me her secret places among the woods.' His words carried more innuendo than he intended, but he decided to leave it there, dangling.

'Her secrets?' Erich repeated sarcastically.

'Thomas has been looking for you,' Ingrid said.

'Well here I am.'

'Here he is,' Ingrid repeated, as if she had delivered one man to the other.

'We need to talk in private,' Thomas said, aware that his shift at work was fast approaching. 'But I have to go now.'

'Why not stay around a bit longer? Stay for a drink. You haven't even finished the sundial yet.' Erich grinned.

'Don't tease,' Ingrid said. 'If he has to go, then he has to go.'

'I have to work this evening.'

'Well, before you go,' Erich said, 'I want to invite you out for dinner. It's Ingrid's birthday in a few days. It's my treat. Bring that girl you've been seeing as well. The one from Potsdam. What's her name?'

'You know her name perfectly well.'

'Yes, you're right. Bring Käthe along. Ingrid would like her to come – that way the numbers will be balanced. How about it?'

'Ok, I'll do that, but we must talk then.'

17

Two mornings later, Thomas left the *Berliner Tageblatt* an hour before dawn and rode on his motorbike directly to Potsdam. He didn't go to see Käthe but to be there at the very instant the clocks of Potsdam struck six. And when they did, he would be stood on the street beneath the terrace, waiting and watching.

It was hearing the clocks at Ingrid's parents' that drew his attention to a new possibility: that the time of day of the boy's descent could be significant. Did something happen in the surroundings at that moment, he wondered? Maybe a regular horse-and-cart was positioned at the foot of the building at that exact hour and could have miraculously broken the boy's fall? Or maybe a laundry van was on its rounds delivering fresh linen and provided the boy with a soft landing? Thomas couldn't help but speculate given there was no trace of blood in the street nor any witnesses. What choice did he have? If he was going to report Erich to the police, then he needed some sort of proof.

Potsdam was as quiet as a whisper when he arrived. He left his bike and walked the last few hundred yards towards Käthe's building. A thin fog lay on the streets, touched orange by the occasional street lamp. He turned up his collar against the chilled morning air and kept watch in all directions. He was alert to the movements of the town. A homeless man trudged beside a brick wall. A black cat prowled in the opposite direction. A milkman carried an aluminium churn on his shoulder.

He reached the foot of Käthe's building and found the shaft where the boy would have fallen. It looked just as familiar as it did from three weeks before. The same pattern of cobblestones, the layers of grime smeared across the top and the sheer vertical brick face.

A few minutes later, the clocks across the town began to chime – the first rings of a new day. He looked around as they struck six o'clock, but to his disappointment, nothing appeared. The street was empty. The corner lay still and inert. It seemed like it had been a wasted journey. He stepped away from the corner and returned to the main street. Minute by minute the dawn light grew stronger.

As he walked on, he crossed a courtyard and entered a long cobbled street. He inhaled the moist morning air as he passed beneath a Gothic brick archway and along another damp passageway. He emerged onto a square with bars and restaurants, all of them shut and silent with their screens lowered like closed eyelids. He began to recognise these streets as those he and Erich had ventured along on their night out in Potsdam, when the bars were lit up like miniature festivals and the violin players and singers lured passersby with their songs.

Then he saw the name of a bar which was stencilled in unlit neon glass against a black background. The name was Clärchens. Then he put his hand into his pocket and drew out the torn slip of paper he'd found at Arno's attic. It dawned on him there and then that he was able to fill in the missing blank now – "Midnight Clärchens." This was where it all began, he thought, as he recognised it as the very same tavern where the thief-boy first approached them. He looked back up at the bar and felt the pieces falling into place. There could be no doubt now: Arno Hiller was in Clärchens tavern at midnight, the exact time he and Erich were there. The note proved it. He must have planned to meet someone in there. But with who? Surely, it was someone he was connected with from Orenstein and Koppel, an old colleague he might depend on for support. No wonder he'd made up the story of living in the hostel above the tavern – it had to be better than the attic room where he lived now.

Just then, a voice from behind him called out. 'Sir, will you spare me a minute?' Thomas turned to find the vagrant approaching. He was a broad shouldered man with a sloping back and a great bulge at the base of his neck. He wore a sort of cape that was riddled with holes, and on his feet a pair of boots held together with black tape.

'Would you spare some change for an old dog like me?'

'Sorry, no.'

'How about you buy this old watch for a few coins then? Just a few coins and I can get myself some food.'

'No – thank you.'

'Not just for a few marks?' At this, the man pulled from his pocket a silver watch and dangled it in the air.

Thomas attempted to walk by.

'It's not stolen,' the vagrant said. 'I found it. Take a look.'

Thomas spent a second looking at the wristwatch to satisfy the man. The glass face was badly cracked and the arms of the clock weren't moving. In all, it was a complete wreck.

'It's broken,' Thomas said. 'It's worthless.'

'Are you sure?'

'Quite sure.'

The man peered at the watch in apparent disbelief.

'Mind you, it's telling the correct time right now.'

'Is it?' Thomas looked again. 'So it is,' he said. The time on the watch agreed with the clocks of town: exactly six o'clock.

Six o'clock?

The watch was fixed at exactly six o'clock.

'Where did you get this from?'

'I told you. I found it.'

'But where did you find it?'

'Somewhere on the other side of the main street as I remember.'

Thomas took hold of the watch and inspected it more closely. Then to his astonishment, he noticed the date on the calendar wheel. It was three weeks before, the exact date of the incident.

It seemed impossible and yet undeniable. Could it be the boy's watch, smashed in the fall and frozen at this precise time?

'You say you found it on the other side town?' Thomas asked again.

'Just lying on the ground it was. I always keep my eyes peeled. You never know what might turn up among the rubbish.'

'But you don't know who it belongs to?'

'I've no idea.' The vagrant rubbed his chin with the back of his hand, pleased that Thomas was taking an interest in his find.

Thomas checked the object over for other signs. He was searching for an engraving, some initials that might confirm or deny Arno Hiller as the owner. There were no distinguishing marks.

Still, it was too remarkable to be a coincidence. The imprint of time that lay frozen in the mechanics of the wristwatch, recording the very moment of impact on the cobbles of Potsdam, was another piece of tangible evidence he had in his possession. It was both a triumph and a mighty blow.

He looked out and saw the town beginning to swell with morning activity, the scurry of hats and overcoats, trams and bicycles. The sunlight came and went, so too the morning traffic, braying horses and the curdled cries of newspaper sellers.

Thomas gave the old vagrant whatever coins he had in his pocket, then returned home on his motorcycle, escorting the broken wristwatch back to Berlin.

THE QUESTION

"How did I come into the world? Why was I not consulted? And if I am compelled to take part in it, where is the director? I want to see him" – Kierkegaard

18

On Tuesday, Beenken turned up in Thomas' room with a new concern. It involved the tenant on the third floor, the same awful fellow that Beenken had been so chummy with just a few days before. According to the old landlord, the man had commandeered a vacant room along the corridor, a room that Beenken had hoped to set aside as a small canteen for the other guests to buy snacks. The rogue tenant had made various threats to Beenken in order to procure the room, including one to slice off his eyelids. After moving in, he'd set up a roulette wheel and a blackjack table, along with an alcove for a fortune-teller, with a curtain partition separating one side from the other.

Beenken was at a loss. He'd attempted to smuggle a locksmith into the building to win the room back, but the tenant – 'That bastard,' as Beenken now called him as a matter of course – caught him in the act. And Beenken was no match for a wooden club and a torrent of insults.

Thomas listened to the woeful narrative. The demeanour of the old boy was difficult to witness, hunched in the corner of the room like a frightened schoolboy.

'How did he get the keys in the first place?'

'That bastard stole them from me. He said he was

going to help me decorate the canteen, so I handed them to him. Then he stole them from me and locked me out.'

'That was rather trusting of you.'

'Yes, Thomas. I know that now. That's why I need your help.'

'But what can I do?' Thomas made an exaggerated gesture to counteract Beenken's pleas.

'Outwit him. I know you can do it. You're the best tenant I have.'

'Really?'

'Oh yes. You're clever. You're good company. You keep your room tidy. I respect you. We all respect you.'

Thomas rolled his eyes at the rally of compliments. He knew Beenken was laying it on thick but he relented anyway.

'Okay, let me think,' he replied.

That same evening he went to work with Beenken's dilemma flitting across his mind. He spent the night working the Linotype slugs at the *Berliner*, his fingers slipping over the morning headlines without attempting to comprehend their meaning.

Then it occurred to him: a way to help Beenken without resorting to quarrelling or violence. Instead, he would attack invisibly, without the bastard even knowing he was being ambushed. And so he made his plan. All he needed was a few nights at the presses without undue attention from his colleagues. Perhaps it could work.

The key would be to give the appearance of normality. If timing and conduct were kept in check, he could make use of the printing room apparatus without raising suspicion. Anyone who saw him might think he was putting in some overtime or else attending to duties beyond his charge. He had access to every stage of the printing process, from the typesetting keyboards to the glyph matrices; he just had to make sure it appeared entirely legitimate that he might be seen using them. His intention was to convince the tenant that he was under suspicion and that the police might call on him at any moment. That should be enough to scare him off.

Thomas had no doubt he could pull it off. His rare ability to appear invisible would help. He was adept at blending in, an expert at slipping in and out of rooms unnoticed. He was not loud or brash, not obnoxious or rude. As such, he tended to give the impression of simple earnestness. At other times this invisibility could be mistaken as shyness; but on this occasion it was surely an advantage.

For one, he was never the subject of suspicion. Once at work, when a piece of machinery broke down, the supervisor made a case for deliberate vandalism. Nearly everyone who came into contact with the machine was interrogated, except for Thomas, who was merely waved away as far too unlikely to be involved.

For another, people tended to trust his word. Once, on his way home from a long shift, he accidentally picked up another man's hat. Every hat in the cloakroom tended to look the same, so it was an easy mistake to make. Except that this particular hat was far superior to Thomas' own ruined item. Not only was it in better condition but it was a great deal more expensive too. Initially, he had no thoughts of keeping it, not until he came to work the next day and bumped into the owner of the hat, who said immediately, 'I use to have a hat like that, until some crook took it. I know it wasn't you.'

'No, I wouldn't do that,' Thomas replied, about to explain the mix-up.

'Didn't think so,' the man apparently not interested in the possible alternative. 'You're just not the type.' At that, he walked away and left Thomas in possession of the hat, which he had worn every day since without ever raising the first hint of suspicion.

So with conditions in his favour, he went about his plan. Over the course of the next four nights, with every edition of the morning paper he constructed a minor variation on the front page, replacing a second-tier story with one of his own invention. All else remained the same: the *Berliner* masthead, the main headline, the array of other stories and bylines across the page. But somewhere on the coversheet, a new item was inserted.

He printed off no more than a dozen copies of this alternative front page. He didn't need to fool the whole city; just one man. Then each morning he took the alternative newspaper back to Beenken and told him what he should do with it.

'Take it to the bastard and make him read this story.' He prodded at the paper with his finger.

Beenken read out the title. '*Berlin police crack down on suburban gambling.*'

'Make him read it,' Thomas said again. 'It's how we can sow the seed in his mind that he's under suspicion.'

'Is it true?' Beenken asked, as his eyes lifted from the page. 'Are the police coming?'

There seemed no point in letting him think otherwise. 'Yes, they're coming.'

'I knew someone would come to my rescue.'

'Just ensure he reads it everyday, so he knows the police are onto him.'

The same thing happened on the following three mornings. Thomas came with a newspaper and gave each one to Beenken. Every day the story headline gained weight and a sense of urgency: *Police closing in on gambling in heart of city.* The next day: *Apartment blocks targeted in illegal casino purge.* The following day: *Dawn raids imminent near the Kurfürstendamm.*

For the news story, Thomas had recycled some old

text from previous reports about criminal and police activity in the city. It was the headlines that counted most of all, and he made sure these wouldn't fail to grab attention.

By the end of the week, he heard a knock on his door. Beenken came in, silent for a moment, lingering. His expression remained like that of a schoolboy, only this time it was a look of purest delight, as if he'd been given a box of chocolates or a small puppy as a gift.

'He's gone,' he announced, his voice lilting with triumph. 'The bastard's gone.'

'He's gone? You mean he gave you your room back?'

'No, he's left entirely. Everything is gone. His rooms are empty, gambling tables and all.'

Thomas smiled and felt relief that the ruse was over with. He waved back at Beenken, suggesting to the landlord that it was time to leave. Beenken retreated, bowing gently in thanks as he did. Thomas couldn't be sure, but he thought he saw a tear brewing in the corner of the old landlord's eye.

19

That evening, the four companions gathered together for their night out in Berlin. They rode in Erich's motorcar, which was surely one of the most expensive on the market. The interior was finished in walnut, glossy and smooth; the upholstery was leather, dyed the colour of beetroot. Ingrid sat beside him, whilst Käthe and Thomas huddled in the back with their hands folded over one another's. On the street, trams whined and horses dragged heavily-laden carts. Music echoed from doorways, ladies appeared adorned in pearls, streetlamps came on, and the car's shining headlamps were two more candles beaming on this luminous city.

Erich's speed was hardly faster than walking pace, but still – absurdly – he wore a pair of leather-trimmed racing goggles whose light brown colour matched the brown corduroy of his raincoat collar. Ingrid beside him wore a dove-coloured beret with three white feathers on the front that trembled and flickered like cinema light. Every move she made was accompanied by the jangle of silver bracelets on both her wrists. It was the sort of outfit that permitted its wearer a degree of eccentricity, or demanded it even. She behaved in an unruly and turbulent manner, not at all like the capricious butterfly she hoped to portray. The following day would be her birthday; she was already drunk, and she intended to attack the midnight hour with impetuous abandon.

Erich sat proudly, with his arms locked straight and his posture upright. He made grand hand-gestures at the city, side-ways glances and puckish grins. To draw attention to his vehicle he shouted out to passers-by – 'Hey, where's your horse?' and 'Watch yourself or I'll run you over!'

Ingrid turned around on her seat and called out to the rear passengers, 'Have I told you that I don't like motorcars? Because in actual fact I hate them. When I see a car hurtling past me I think awful thoughts. I think about the driver spinning into a ditch as punishment for going so fast.'

Käthe turned to Thomas and laughed. She loved motorcars, she said. 'I wish my father could see me now, he would be jealous up to his eyeballs.'

Ingrid turned around again – 'And I hate trains too. They are just moving factories making dirty smoke. I don't like them one bit and I don't think they like me either!' She laughed in an absurd sort of way, then without pausing began to sing in a bright voice that was pretty but did nothing to placate Erich and only made the other passengers feel uncomfortable. The group had shared three bottles of wine over as hastily consumed dinner and Ingrid had drunk more than her fair share.

Shortly after, Erich pulled the car up beside the pavement and the party got out to travel on foot. The night was warm, the warmest of the year so far. Battalions of night-goers uncoiled across the pavement in spirals. Theatres and cabarets opened their doors and a festive air seeped out into the night air.

On Ingrid's orders, the group went into a bar named *Liebeserklaerung*. 'This place is such a scream!' she called out as they entered. Thomas looked around him, noticing how all the tables were set in booths backed with wooden panels, and on each panel a telephone was fastened.

'All you have to do is dial the number,' Ingrid explained, grabbing Thomas' arm. 'If you want, you can call up someone on the other side of the room. You can declare your love to them if your heart tells you.'

Each table was marked by a brass number, which was the telephone number for that table. Suggested chat-up lines were painted in bright red and orange on the walls. The *Liebeserklaerung* was principally a haunt for tourists, and in the summer months, when Berlin was full of out-of-towners, it was riotous with every shade of prank or serious flirtation. When, however, tourism slowed during the winter months, a more solemn crowd made it their home. Amid a rather anxious air of desperation, one didn't have to search too hard to find a genuine lonely-heart, sipping watered-down cocktails and waiting patiently for the shrill invitation of a telephone bell.

For fun, Ingrid and Thomas sat together in one booth whilst Käthe and Erich sat across the room from them in another. After about three minutes the telephone rang and Thomas answered. It was Käthe. She put on a coquettish voice and asked if he'd like to buy her a drink, promising that if he did she would be more than happy to start a liaison with him. Sometime later, Erich telephoned Ingrid and made her laugh by mimicking an old man, who slurped on his tongue and made crude suggestions into the mouthpiece.

The couples then swapped over. Now Ingrid and Käthe were sat on one table while Erich and Thomas sat on another.

This was Thomas' chance, as if the weeks of angst had been building towards this specific opportunity. He told Erich to listen closely. He spoke quickly in order to have his say. 'I found out something,' he said. 'Käthe has a brother. He's called Arno and he was at the apartment that night.'

'Which night?' Erich asked lightly.

At that moment the phone began to ring. Erich reached over and picked it up, before Thomas grabbed it from him and flung it onto the table.

'That night we were there, on the terrace in Potsdam.'

'Yes, yes, I know.' Erich gave a leisurely smile.

'Arno!' Thomas said. 'He's Käthe's younger brother. I know for a fact that he was there. You remember the boy who approached us in the bar? That was him.'

'Käthe's brother? Are you sure?'

Thomas pulled out the torn slip of paper with the half-legible note written on it. 'I found this and worked it out.'

'What's that?'

'I found it at Arno's apartment. He was due to meet someone at Clärchens bar at midnight and in looking for them, he found us instead and asked if we were from Orenstein and Koppel.'

'You found this at his apartment? Did you break in?'

'That's irrelevant,' Thomas said. 'Listen to me Erich, nobody has seen him in months.'

'Yes, I know about Arno.'

'You know?'

'I know she has a brother. But the rest is conjecture.'

'You know him?'

'I didn't say that. I know of him. We've never actually met before.'

Thomas glared at his friend.

'Relax Thomas,' Erich said. 'Really, is this the right time for all of this conversation? I'm here to enjoy myself. Why ruin it with speculation?'

Thomas went on, 'It's not speculation. I found some broken spectacles on the terrace just like the pair the boy was wearing. Käthe confirmed they belong to her brother and she showed me that they were engraved with his initials. And then I came across this watch.' Thomas took the broken wristwatch from his pocket. 'Look at the time and date on it. That's the exact time the boy fell from the terrace. It has to be his.'

'Thomas, this conversation is boring me. I want to make a telephone call now.'

'Do you remember that story you told me about the soldier who returned home only for his mother and sister to bludgeon him to death? Well, that's what we did. We made a mistake. *You* made a mistake. You killed him by mistake. And it was Arno.'

Erich paused on the notion, his eyes drifting away to a distance thought. 'Yes, it's possible I suppose.'

'Is that it? It's *possible*? But what if it's true? This must be put in the hands of the law.'

'The problem is that you care too much,' Erich said. 'You are modest and courageous at the same time, Thomas. That's why we all like you. You always want to see justice done.'

'I'm not interested in your riddles tonight, Erich. I want you to admit what you've done and take some responsibility.'

'You should be interested, because your choices will make all the difference,' Erich said cryptically.

Suddenly Thomas felt he was hearing something absolutely truthful for the first time in weeks. He looked at Erich. 'I have to do the right thing. You may not understand that, but the police need to know about Arno. I'm sorry.'

Erich's smile twitched. 'So we must leave each other?'

'One of us has to tell the truth about what happened, even if that means you have to face the consequences.'

'You'd do that, would you Thomas?'

'How can we not say anything? What happened was murder.'

'Well, I'm glad of one thing,' Erich said after a long pause. 'That you have made a decision at last.'

'That's what I must to do. Friend or not Erich, you have taken a life.'

'So you know the truth do you?'

'Can you provide another explanation?'

'No, and if you can't ignore your conscience, then please yourself. But truth? I'm not so sure you're in possession of that.'

'Damn you Erich, I've had enough of this charade.' Thomas spoke angrily as he lifted his closed fist, as if to strike Erich there and then.

'I wouldn't do that, if I were you,' Erich said.

Thomas scowled at his friend for a moment, then picked up the phone from the table and put it back onto the receiver. As he did, he pressed the phone to his ear for a moment and thought he heard the click of a phone being hung up at the other end. Surely someone hadn't been listening? He stood up and walked back to Käthe and Ingrid's table.

'Your phone has been engaged for ages,' Ingrid said, beginning to slur.

'It must be broken,' Thomas replied humourlessly.

Just then, the phone next to Ingrid began to ring. Thomas made it his business to answer it.

'What?'

'Is she annoying you?' Erich asked down the line.

'Who?'

'Ingrid. If she is, just lift her up and drop her over the side of the table. You might even feel better for it.

141

I'm not joking, she's a mess! See how she smokes cigarettes one after another just to make herself more giddy? And did you see how much wine she drank over dinner?'

'You make quite a pairing.'

'Yes, I know. But if she's trying to catch up with me, she has a long way to go.'

Thomas put the phone down and turned to Ingrid, who had by now slumped to one side. She was not the same girl he had made sundials with just a week before. He knew how she loved to have fun, to put on voices and sing. But tonight she was drunk beyond anything he recognised as pleasurable.

'We should get her out of here,' Käthe said, reading Thomas' thoughts.

Just at that moment, he noticed something going on at the entrance to the *Liebeserklaerung*. Evidently it was some kind of fracas. A man was pushed up against a door, whereupon the door collapsed open and the man fell through into the street. A modest brawl broke out onto the edge of the pavement.

The four friends stood up to see. 'This doesn't look good,' Käthe whispered to Thomas.

Outside, the brawl staggered left and right, and rose up like three bears fighting, crumpled and rummaged in the gutter. The three men fought in an untidy ball, one of them a policeman, another a soldier, and the other a heavily bearded man who wore no discernable uniform except for a blazer that suggested he belonged to some kind of fraternity.

The hoard of bystanders looked on in a state of confusion; the spectacle was at once comic and frightening. Just then, the man with the beard drew out a knife and took a swipe at the soldier. The policeman found his feet and came forward, this time with his baton in hand, landing a firm strike on the side of the bearded man's head. The policeman leered over him in triumph. The bearded man passed his eyes across the crowd and then took the absurd step of arranging the knife against his very own wrist. His hands began to shake, the knife erect in his hand, held hard against his other wrist. All of a sudden – in the same manner as a guitar string snaps when it is stretched too far – he cast the knife into the road and let out a wild and painful laugh, a laugh that was like fire, and in this way, attempted to blame the sheer madness of it all on those around him.

He rolled limply over onto his front then over again onto his back, raising his legs and screaming in a combination of delight and derision. His hands were close up to his chest and his fingers were pointing at the crowd. He was laughing and hooting like a fallen drunk. The colour ran away from his face and the tension in his body quickly unwound. Immediately the policeman leapt over and landed flush on top of him, and with the help of some of the spectators, pulled him to his feet and escorted him down the street.

Only after a few moments did Thomas realise that one of the spectators leading the bearded man away was Erich. He dashed after the huddle and called Erich's name.

'Erich, where are you going?'

'They're taking him to the police station,' Erich replied. 'I'm helping to restore order.'

Erich did not pause to explain further. He hurried after the wounded man and the posse of keepers that surrounded him, and Thomas, somewhat baffled with the turn of events, was left in the middle of the street.

Moments later, Käthe came up behind and whispered into Thomas' ear that Ingrid was ready to go

143

home. He agreed, so together they helped her onto a passing tram. Presuming himself now compelled to treat Ingrid better than Erich had done, Thomas dropped Käthe off at the appropriate stop on the way, and then sat with Ingrid as the tram rattled through the city night towards her apartment.

20

'Why must I always make up for my friend's shortcomings?' Thomas thought to himself as he and Ingrid sat on the tram. Ingrid began to sober up and it wasn't long before she sensed Erich was not with them. When she realised this, she began to speak in apologetic terms.

'Sorry you've been the one left to take me home. Where did Erich go off to? Is he coming back?'

'He's chosen to vanish and play the role of the upstanding citizen,' Thomas said with an air of disdain.

'Erich has been disappearing a lot just recently. He stays out late, don't ask me with who. He gets picked up in a dark coloured motorcar at night and when he comes home, he's often agitated.'

'Does he tell you where he goes?'

'He says he's been out playing cards and has lost too much money!' she said as the tram suddenly shook. 'Oh dear, I think I drank far too much.'

'We'll be home soon,' Thomas said.

'Is it my fault?' Ingrid went on. 'He's tired of me isn't he? I should be more generous with him. Is that what he wants from me?'

'I really think we should both forget about Erich for tonight.' By now his anger at Erich's behaviour had turned into a grotesque form of foreboding.

'No, I don't want to forget about him. I feel sorry for him.'

'This isn't the time to feel sorry for him Ingrid,' Thomas said. 'You're tired.'

'Look at me! I'm a state!'

'We're not far now.'

The pair remained silent as the suburbs of Berlin rolled by through the darkened windows. Ingrid kept her eyes open and stared straight ahead of her. Some time passed before she spoke again, this time in more articulate tones.

'Can you remember the war?'

'Of course.'

'Did I ever tell you what happened to me?'

'No.'

'My father was a surgeon. Did I ever tell you that? He has stopped working now, but when the war was on he was extremely busy. He worked from home. Men with wounds would come round to visit him as part of their recuperation. Officers, higher-ranking soldiers – he would examine them, replace stitches and often perform small operations. He had all the instruments at home, you see, along with supplies of morphine, all locked away in a box. Do you know what morphine is?'

'Yes.'

'My father kept a large stock of it for the wounded soldiers. He would give it to all the men he treated and sometimes he would give it to me. Are you surprised? You look a little shocked, but morphine is okay. Here, take my hand, see I'm not ill.' She looked up and smiled.

'But why did you take it?'

'Because when I was about twelve, I was regularly in pain – that is not an easy time for a girl. So you see, that's why my father gave me the drug, to comfort me.'

'And do you still take it?'

146

'I suppose I never really stopped taking it. Actually, that's not true. It's only now and then. I enjoy it but it's not so easy to get anymore, not now my father has stopped treating others. I used to take his prescription forms, you see. But now it's not that easy. I speak to doctors and the nice ones give it to me, thank God. Anyway, I don't know why I started talking about it. Is it time to get off this tram yet, we must be nearly home by now?'

They arrived at Ingrid's apartment at a quarter to midnight. They sat together in her living room waiting for the coming of the hour. It was a strange way to go about celebrating a birthday. As twelve o'clock approached they exchanged fewer and fewer words until, with two minutes to go, they stopped speaking altogether. Ingrid's mind was many miles away, and when the chimes from the clock in the hallway rang, her eyes filled with tears that ran in streaks down her face. The sound of her crying filled the room, and for a time Thomas felt overcome with pity.

Ingrid went into the hall and sobbed in muffled tones at the door. As the hour passed, she and Thomas conversed a little, but he could say nothing to fully pacify her. He left shortly after one o'clock. As he went to leave, she kissed him on the cheek and thanked him. Then, in an unexpected turn, she came forward and took hold of his hand. She gave it a short tug back in the direction of the living room, intimating another choice as her eyes looked straight into his. Her lips parted slightly for just a moment, making an assertion, one which Thomas understood instantly. He hesitated on the edge of a situation he had not imagined.

She held her demeanour for a moment longer, waiting for a response. Thomas said nothing and could only think about Käthe. When Ingrid realised he was not about to consent, her face seemed to relax and she returned to a more reticent composure.

'Thomas,' she called after him as he left.

'Yes?'

'Thank you again – for staying with me.'

'That's alright.'

'Has Erich mentioned that I'm going to have a baby?'

'A baby? No, he didn't mention it.'

'Isn't that why you stayed to look after me?'

'I stayed because we're friends. I didn't know you were pregnant.'

'Well I am. What do you think about that?'

'I don't know. I really don't know what to think. I wonder why you would drink so much if you knew you're carrying a baby?'

'Aren't you happy for us?'

He thought for a second. 'Of course. I'm shocked – but of course I'm happy for you.' He stepped forward and kissed her on the forehead. 'I'm delighted, congratulations.'

'I don't know what will happen,' she said.

'Everything will be fine. Now, you must go to bed. Take a drink of water with you.'

'I will. I've stopped crying now. See?'

Thomas let the door close quietly behind him as Ingrid went back inside. His journey home was slow and pensive. Most of the trams had ceased for the night, so he had to walk half the journey back. As he went, he took heed of the further disarray he saw before him and realised he now had a much more difficult decision to make.

21

As a new morning opened up, Thomas lay in his bed contemplating the news of Ingrid's pregnancy and how it would affect him going to the police. Could it be? What will become of her and Erich now? What kind of a father will he make, especially if he goes to prison…?

He analysed the situation coolly. 'As soon as Erich is arrested for his crime…' he said to himself. Then all at once, his blood chilled as a single realisation overtook all others. Was he not paralysed now? For how could he proceed to seek justice for one life without compromising another – the second of which wasn't even born yet? He sifted through the thought, knowing with terrible resignation how Ingrid's pregnancy would act as Erich's protection. How could he go to the police now? The image he had taken time to conceive, to bring his friend before the machinery of the law and see him bow down in repentance, was dissolving before his mind's eye.

He pressed his head back into his pillow, feeling ambivalent and worn. As he lay there, looking up at the ceiling with its bloom of mould spots and flaking paint, he thought about Erich's apartment. It was the contrast that prompted his train of thought, the wretched contrast between his shabby room and Erich's palatial suite.

He thought back to the last time he'd been there, before any of the recent adversities had put a divide between them. On the surface, he went there to return a copy of a Baudelaire text Erich had lent him, but he also went just to spend a brief time in the palm of luxury. It turned out to be an interesting day, one which had connotations that he was only now beginning to pick up.

It was a Sunday afternoon. He recalled being stood at Erich's door, a lavish oak-panelled entrance with iron metalwork. Erich answered wearing one of his expensive jackets made of finely woven wool, tailored long and oversized. His hair was slicked back and he wore a capricious smile.

'Thomas! My old sidekick. What a surprise! I was just heading out. But please, come inside!'

As the pair walked through to the living area, Erich picked up a glass of whiskey from the sideboard. In the living room Thomas handed him the Baudelaire.

'Marvellous. Did you enjoy it?'

'I've read it. I doubt there is a book more suited to our city. I was inspired.' Thomas spoke with enthusiasm. He was especially impressed with the poet's image of the *flâneur*, a man who roamed the city with his eyes wide open, a connoisseur of urban life who could see the whole world in the upturned face of a busy street.

Erich held up his glass tumbler. 'Shall I get you one too? We must do this properly. Do you want it on its own or will you be wanting something to soften the taste?'

Thomas agreed to drink his whiskey straight. Erich went to fetch a tumbler whilst at the same time leading his guest to the large window at the rear of the apartment, where a great expanse of light opened over the green trees of the Tiergarten park.

'This is some view, we will miss this,' he declared.

'You will miss this view, won't you Thomas?'

Erich's tone took Thomas by surprise. 'Miss the view? Why, are you going somewhere?'

'Not that I know of. But who knows what is around the next corner. Isn't that right?'

'I thought for a minute you were going to tell me you were leaving Berlin.'

'Berlin? Never. This is the centre of the universe.'

'Quite right.'

'Have you eaten? I'll fetch some plates for us – come with me to the kitchen.'

They walked through the large apartment with its superlative views. The other windows were tall and elegant, flanked by long red curtains stitched with patterns of Persian flora. A grand leather armchair kept watch over the city, attended by an oak reading-table on one side and a tall, carved bookcase on the other.

The fineness of the apartment was all thanks to the wealth of Erich's family. His father ran two large factories and planned to open a third soon. A resourceful businessman, he had escaped the tumultuous start to the decade with profit-based speculations abroad, just as the German currency was tumbling in value. Now the dividends of that success were decorating Erich's apartment.

'Are you all set for the trip to Potsdam?' he asked. 'Next week, remember, we're all being cast for the portrait.'

'Yes, I'm ready,' Thomas replied.

'The artist has a growing reputation for her painting style.' Erich's face sparkled.

Thomas didn't respond, aware that he hadn't seen any of the artist's work.

'Come on Thomas! She's one of Berlin's greatest living painters! A little more enthusiasm please!'

'Is she really that good? I've never heard of her.'

'Well, that's because you live at the blunt end of culture. I, on the other hand, exist only at its sharpest point.'

'Is that so?' Thomas remarked, laughing.

'You will see, when she holds her next exhibition, how highly regarded she is. And you will be making a star appearance. Your face will be on the gallery walls.'

'Yes, I imagine it will, what a prospect!'

'Go with the flow Thomas. These are good times for us. Thanks to me.'

Thomas acknowledged Erich's self-congratulations. 'So, is that why you called me over?' he asked, raising his glass to his lips.

'There's something else… I wanted to speak to you about it. I've been meaning to for days now.'

'Go on.'

'Only, I happened to do something quite stupid recently. Quite foolish, even for me.'

'What is it?'

'I went to the area around the west of the park. It's… notorious. Do you know it? Probably not.'

'I do actually,' Thomas interrupted.

'And do you know what a man can find down there?'

'There are plenty of brothels there.'

'Yes, that's right,' Erich smiled gently, granting Thomas his insight. 'Well, I was there, not for any purpose, curiosity really. It's hard to explain. I wanted to see the conditions – do you understand?'

'The conditions?'

'When I was there, I started talking to one of the girls. She was suspicious of me at first but eventually she told me of the hardship and suffering that goes on there. I began to feel sorry for her. She didn't care about my pity of course, but I couldn't help it.'

Thomas listened. It seemed strange to hear Erich talk in this way. He expected him to speak of 'cleaning up the sickness' or 'knocking the whole district down' or something to that usual effect, not this tone of compassion.

'I offered her some money,' Erich went on. 'No strings, I didn't want anything in return. I just offered her a hand-full of notes. And she took it.' He stopped, plotting his next words carefully. 'Then I told her where I live. I gave her the address for this place and said she could sleep here whenever she wanted. The thing is, she actually turned up and has been staying here for the last three nights.'

'You're joking?'

'No. Nothing happened. That wasn't my intention. I just felt concerned for her welfare. She told me she sleeps on the streets some nights. That's why I took her in.'

'So she's living here with you now?' Thomas said, glancing around the apartment.

'No, no, she doesn't live here. She left this morning, but she can't come back. It has to end. It was a whim. I was taken in, quite thoughtless on my part really. It's too dangerous. If Ingrid found out, or any of the family, there would be total outrage. I'd have an impossible time explaining it. So I have to put a stop to it. Today.'

'Today?'

'Come with me Thomas. We'll go and find her together.' Already Erich was taking a coat from a cupboard and putting his arms through the sleeves.

'I didn't anticipate this!'

'I have to get this sorted out. Come and help me fix it.'

Erich led his friend down to the street. After twenty minutes of walking, they turned a corner into a rough cobblestone lane. There were rows of torn posters along one wall and half the windows were boarded up. Thomas glanced about him expectantly. He remembered when he first moved to Berlin, how he'd stumbled across this neighbourhood unintentionally. He recalled there were women all along the street that day. One of them whistled at him and another attempted to beckon him over, but he kept on walking.

Today the street was empty. Then, after a minute or two, a young boy of about nine or ten came running out of a doorway. There was a skip in his step and a flush of eagerness in his face. He ran up to the two men and with great urgency grabbed hold of Thomas' raincoat sleeve and pulled on it forcibly.

'Come with me sir,' he said in a rapid tongue. 'Come on sir… this way… take a look… anything you want sir… I've got a sister… have you got money on you, sir?… It won't cost you much… just follow me… come on sir… I'll be in trouble if you don't… won't take up much of your time… she's a real flower… follow me, sir.'

Thomas watched wide-eyed as the boy circled him. Fearless and insolent with it, the boy soon moved onto Erich, who was altogether more delighted with the attention.

'How about you sir?… want to follow me?… we've got whatever you want this afternoon.'

Erich laughed. Then he said, 'I'm looking for Gina? Is she around?' He spoke in the sort of light, belittling tone that adults enjoy to use on children. 'I've got plenty of money.'

'Whatever you're after. Wait here a minute…' The boy ran back through the door and disappeared inside. The two men waited in silence until the boy re-emerged, this time with company. A young girl stepped out from the shadows. Her pale grey eyes squinted in the light. She wore a white cotton dress that was tightly fitted and that had been sewn up to reveal her boots and laced-up black stockings. Around her neck hung a pathetic looking fox-stole and on her head a red fur bonnet that covered most of her hair. She crossed her arms over her chest in something of a defiant pose. The boy ran up to Erich again and pulled on his sleeve.

'That's not Gina,' Erich said. 'Go and find me Gina. Do you understand?'

'I don't know any Gina,' the boy said.

'Fetch me Gina now,' Erich commanded.

'I don't know any Gina,' the boy said, more trenchantly this time.

At this, the woman said something that neither of the men could make out. Thomas began walking towards her, thinking he would enquire about the whereabouts of Gina himself, but without much ado she retreated back into the shadow of the doorway and left the boy to his patter. Just then, a second woman came through the entryway and stood in the light.

'Is that Gina?' Thomas asked Erich.

'No,' he said, shaking his head. 'That's not her either.'

The second woman was dressed very much the same as the first, though she was much taller and had a leaner face with angled features.

'Come inside,' she called over in a strong voice. Thomas and Erich went towards her and in through the doorway.

Inside they entered a room with wine-coloured walls and threadbare rugs on the floor. There were no windows; the darkness was lit by several gas lamps positioned on tables around the room. In the middle was a circular divan and on it were three young women,

155

gathered like mannequins in a shop display. They all wore lace dresses with semi-transparent fabric and long necklaces of beads and pearls. They began to act flirtatiously as the two men entered. Thomas caught sight of his reflection in one of the many mirrors that lined the walls.

Erich was the first to speak. 'I am looking for Gina.'

At this, an older woman appeared into the room. She was heavily made-up and was wearing a black silk dressing gown and white stockings on her feet. 'Gina?' she said as she went to one of the tabletop lamps and turned up the flame.

'That's right,' Erich said. 'I believe she works here.'

'There is nobody of that name here, but we have plenty of other girls for you to choose from.'

Erich passed his eyes over the three girls on the divan. They posed and purred as his gaze landed on them. One of them grinned, revealing a smile with three teeth missing.

'No, it's Gina I'm looking for.'

Thomas watched on. He noticed there were an uncommon number of doors leading off from the room – and guessed they opened into bedrooms for their paying gentlemen.

'Come on Thomas, we're wasting our time here.' Erich turned to leave the room.

'Wait,' the older woman said. 'This is Gina.' She gave a quick wave of her hand towards one of the girls, who promptly stood up. 'Gina? Why don't you make these gentlemen comfortable.'

Thomas glanced to Erich. It was clear that this wasn't Gina, and he thought the attempt to deceive them might anger Erich. But Erich responded otherwise. 'Gina, you are very lovely,' he said in a soft voice, 'but I'm looking for someone else. Now please sit down.' At

156

this, Erich walked away and left the room.

'She's not here, then?' Thomas concluded as they stepped back out onto the empty street.

'No,' Erich said in a rather vague way.

'They don't seem to have heard of Gina,' Thomas said. 'Isn't that strange?'

'Maybe, but I imagine girls come and go from here all the time.'

'So perhaps she's gone.'

'Yes, let's hope so! Perhaps I have nothing more to worry about.'

Erich never made mention of Gina again and that seemed to be the end of the matter.

As Thomas lay in his bed and let the memory of that day roll around his mind, he wondered what the real purpose was for Erich taking him to find the girl. Did she even exist? After all, Erich could have gone there by himself as he did originally. Something else was going on that day, but for now Thomas couldn't for the life of him see what it was.

Just then, a loud snort came from the opposite corner of the room. Malik was sleeping and had begun to snore. His foot was sticking out from the bedclothes, twitching wildly. His big toe carried a huge red blister. Even a drifter like him has to sleep – Thomas thought. And Malik was the prince of sleep. He could manage twelve hours without breaking his stride and had been known to stay in bed for fifteen or sixteen hours on his very best days.

Thomas got out of bed and pushed his head through the drapes. The sky was a grey mist and the air hung in a damp pall. On the rooftop opposite he saw a large bundle of twigs marking the site of a crows's nest.

It began to rain and a cloak of shifting grey covered

the long avenue. Looking down, he noticed something on the ground, right beneath his window. It was just where old Beenken had been scrubbing away at the swastika sign that had been painted in black on the pavement.

He had thought Beenken had washed it all away, but now with the rain making the ground wet, the sign seemed to be resurfacing. He could see its hooked arms emerging from the gloom, a ghost of the emblem rising out of the stone and dirt.

Then as Thomas looked closer, something dawned on him. In Potsdam, when he stood on the fire escape looking down to the street, he'd seen the same thing! Only then, he'd perceived it to be the hooked limb and the bent arm of a human being. He thought he'd seen the silhouette of a body on the ground. Maybe it was no imprint of a body at all but in fact a painted swastika, a daubed symbol brought back to life when the rain fell.

He was astonished. Had he wanted to see a body when there wasn't one? Yet, he'd seen the boy go over, that wasn't an invention. He saw it happen before his eyes. Still, the realisation of the swastika on the street gave him the strangest feeling, that nothing was quite as it seemed.

He stepped back from the window and opened the drapes to let the light in, at which Malik gave a loud groan and pulled his bedsheets over his head.

22

The next day, Thomas rode his motorbike to Potsdam to collect Käthe, who had a further sitting with the painter Jana Constein at her studio in Wilmersdorf district. When he arrived, he found Käthe already waiting on the street for him. He was happy to see her. It was as if she was an antidote to all his shadowy concerns over Erich.

As she approached, he instantly noticed something different about her. As she drew closer, he saw that she'd had her hair cut. She no longer had the lengthy cascade of locks he'd first encountered but a much shorter bob haircut, cropped and scored in sharp lines and then waxed closely to the shape of her head.

'Your hair!' he exclaimed.

'I had it done this morning. I wanted to have something more sophisticated and bold. Do you like it?'

He grinned. She looked quite different, and somehow more remarkable. 'I do. I think you look modern and charming all at once.'

'I'm glad,' she said excitedly as she climbed onto the back of the motorbike.

It took twenty minutes to ride to the studio for her second sitting, which was also to be her last. The artist's method, to add each figure in turn, meant that the great painting was being slowly populated from one side of the canvas to the other, and Käthe's turn was almost

159

complete.

On the way, with her arms locked around his torso, they chatted and took in the city. The greyness of the morning had now lifted. A summer haze rested on the rooftops and the shop windows glinted with sunlight reflections. Thomas enjoyed the feeling of Käthe's arms wrapped around him, as the newly born sun warmed their shoulders and the passing air swept across them both.

At Wilmersdorf, he dropped her off at the foot of the artist's building where he would pick her up again later. He bought a copy of the *Berliner* to read, and then found a bench in a nearby park. He opened the pages of the newspaper and found the bold headlines gave the usual cause for alarm, much like every other day of the week. He read about a financial scandal involving some high-ranking politician implicated in a corruption plot. There was a story next to it claiming more political dishonesty, where parliamentary votes were said to have been deliberately miscounted. Further inside, there were stories of increasing prostitution across the city and a lengthy article about organised crime: thirteen mysterious kidnappings in the past fortnight proved that underworld activity was rife.

Once he finished the newspaper, he let the distasteful stories slip from his mind and made his way to meet Käthe. As he waited for her, he imagined her sitting for Jana. He remembered the pose she adopted on that day in Potsdam, with her spine kinked and her head tilted as she gazed across the rooftops from the balustrade. He thought how beautiful she was, and more than that, he admired her independent spirit and how she was so alert to the city culture and its artistic scene. He wondered if the artist was taking her on a guided tour of her paintings, looking through dozens of canvases one by one. He realised the idea appealed to him, as it was deemed to be a privilege to be shown around the artist's workspace.

When Käthe emerged, she was beaming. She told him she'd enjoyed herself immensely, even if her pose had brought some discomfort to her lower back, which she bent back and forth to ease its stiffness. Thankfully, a good-natured determination on her part saw her through the two-hour session. And her new haircut had not phased the artist one bit, in fact she was very complimentary.

Then, out of the blue, she asked Thomas, 'Will you take me to see my brother?'

'Your brother Arno?' Thomas asked taken aback.

'Let's go round to his apartment and surprise him. You'd like to meet him wouldn't you? It's so much easier to get there on your motorbike.'

Thomas scratched his neck behind his ear. 'If you really want to,' he said. 'Do you think he'll be there?'

'There's no telling with Arno, but we can try. It'll be fun to pay him a visit.'

Thomas agreed to ride to Hallesches Tor. Of course, he'd been there before but Käthe knew nothing about that – so he would have to act as if it was the first time. What they would find there he didn't know, but he could only suspect that Käthe's brother would not be there.

Within ten minutes they were dismounting the motorbike and looking up at Arno's building. Käthe led the way, past the broken elevator and towards the staircase.

'We have to get to the fifth floor first but let's see if his key is in its usual place.'

She went to the cupboard where Thomas knew the electrical box was stored, and just as he had done some weeks before, she reached her arm behind the wooden casing in search of the key.

Then she gave a yell. 'Oh my god,' she said retracting her hand.

'What is it?' Then he remembered the dead rat. It must still be there. She stepped back and nestled herself against Thomas' side.

'Let me get the key,' he said, before reaching into the cupboard himself. He prodded around and moved his fingers in the darkness, gathering up dust and cobwebs under his fingernails, but there was no sign of the key. It didn't make sense. He tried to remember if he'd replaced the key exactly where he found it when he came here last. He thought back – yes he did. He'd made a particular point of returning it to the very same spot so to appear undisturbed.

'There's nothing here,' he said turning to Käthe.

'Well, that proves it. He must be upstairs then. That's good news.'

Thomas forced a smile.

'Between you and me,' she said, 'I had begun to worry about him. It's been more than a month since I last saw or heard anything from him.'

Thomas was perplexed. Perhaps he had got everything wrong? And he remembered the daubed swastika he'd seen Beenken scrubbing from the street. With the memory, he felt the faintest hope that Arno was upstairs and not the boy on the roof terrace after all.

Käthe led the way up the staircase. As she went, she described how Arno had lived in the attic for more than a year. 'As you'll see, it's quite basic living quarters but he seems to like it. I'd prefer it if he could find somewhere better but I think it's all that he can afford.'

Thomas tried to listen attentively but all he could really think of was finally meeting her brother and feeling the bone-shuddering relief that he was, in fact, alive.

162

When they reached the fifth floor, Käthe pointed along the corridor to the wooden steps that led up to the attic space. 'It's just up here.'

Thomas could see the attic hatch was open. He looked at Käthe and noticed she was about to call up to alert her brother to their presence. Quickly he put his finger to her lips. 'Shsshh. Let's surprise him,' he said in a whisper. He was aware that he might be seen by the neighbour he'd spoken to when he was last there.

'That's a good idea,' Käthe replied. She was excited. She took the steps slowly so as not to make a noise, with Thomas following behind just as gingerly.

He wondered if this was the moment where everything could change for him and Käthe. If Arno was alive, maybe all of those questions could be put into the past. He began to think he could then love Käthe freely and honestly, without all the alarming mystery with Erich and the roof terrace twisting his judgement.

Käthe climbed through the hatch and up into the room. A moment later, Thomas was stood next to her. The room was empty.

'I don't understand,' Käthe said confusedly.

The only things in the room were the objects Thomas had seen before: the bicycle with a flat tyre, the line of washing strung from one side of the room to the other, and the collection of empty beer bottles in the corner. It was exactly as he remembered it, right down to the pair of socks pegged on the line.

'It does seem strange,' Thomas replied. Of course, it was no surprise that Arno was nowhere to be seen; but with the hatch open, somebody else must have been there.

'He wouldn't just leave his room unlocked like this,' Käthe said.

Thomas looked around and suddenly stepped

forward, noticing something on the floor. He dipped his head beneath the washing line and crossed the room towards the bed. There was an object under the bed frame that he was sure wasn't there before. He bent down and picked up a fancy book of matches. On the front was the word *Beguine* printed in fine writing.

He was right, somebody had been here and he knew exactly who it could be.

'What is it?' Käthe asked.

He didn't know how to answer. There was only one person he knew who frequented the Beguine Bar and that was Erich Ostwald. It was one of those dimly lit places where the tables were packed tightly together and cigarette smoke hung on the air like a fog. Erich went there for the jazz music and the black singers who wore shimmering dresses and crooned passionately on the elaborately adorned stage.

Why would Erich have been to Arno's room? Thomas could only think that Erich had begun to join the jots as he had done. What had he come for? Was he trying to cover his tracks in some way?

Thomas handed the matchbook to Käthe.

'It looks like my brother has been enjoying himself,' she said, reaching a different conclusion.

Thomas felt his heart sink at her misinterpretation.

'Shall we wait for him?' she said. 'He may be back soon.'

'Do you think we should linger?' Thomas asked, knowing it would be hopeless to do so.

'You didn't mind coming here, did you?' she asked.

'Not at all.'

She noticed he was beginning to act a little strange. 'Is there something the matter?'

In that moment, he wanted to tell her everything. About Erich and Arno, about having been to the attic room before, about the watch he had found in Potsdam, and about Ingrid's baby too. He wanted to share everything.

'I think I could do with a drink. Maybe I could meet Arno some other time. We don't know when he may return.'

They left the attic and went down for coffee at Café Kaiser on the ground floor. 'I'm going to put an advertisement in a newspaper,' Käthe declared as they sat down. 'I've made a decision, I want to place a missing persons advert in the next print run. Somebody must know something about where Arno is. I've seen adverts like that before, in the *Tempo*. They seem to advertise missing people more and more these days. And what with Arno mislaying his spectacles, and now his room key missing, and with no trace of him, I'm beginning to worry more.'

Thomas nodded gravely.

'And if I haven't heard anything in a week's time, I'm going to the police.'

Thomas tried to agree but the temptation to tell her everything he knew was tremendous. He resisted and held his breath, for he knew that he needed to get to the truth himself before he could reveal it to her.

'I hope,' he said as he gripped Käthe's hand, 'we can find your brother soon. Arno must be found.'

THE ANSWER

"After such knowledge, what forgiveness?" – T. S. Eliot

23

Through the following week, Thomas kept an eye on the newspapers. Each morning, he went down to the vendor across the street and skimmed through the pages of the *Tempo*, looking for Käthe's advert. He found nothing, no mention of Arno. He decided she must have changed her mind – or had hesitated in acting on her decision. Whatever the reason, it seemed to buy him more time to resolve the question himself.

He resumed the rhythms of his work, the late-night and early morning back and forth to the printing rooms. As for Käthe, he heard nothing from her. In that silence, he began to feel it was almost a reprieve. It was impossible to untangle his feelings for her from the fear of what may have happened to her brother. He knew he was falling in love with her, but it was a love fraught with unknown consequences.

Now it was his turn to visit to Jana Constein's studio in Wilmersdorf and have his sitting. He climbed the stairwell up to the fourth floor and approached her studio. After knocking and receiving no answer, he pushed on the door and entered a lively and hectic scene. The room appeared all at once like a trove, with artists' brushes and tubes of paint everywhere, gleaming with the lustre of an altogether distinctive occupation.

Then Jana appeared. 'Thomas, thank you for

journeying over. Please do come in.' She was wearing a painter's smock and around her neck a knotted red neckerchief made of silk. Behind her, he could see the studio area lit generously with light that spread evenly and pleasingly throughout. A plug-in gramophone played an American jazz record that echoed through the room.

He made his way into the studio, stepping over boxes and props. A bottle of distilled turpentine sweetened the air with a sugary, petroleum-like smell. The same scent lurked over a large box of oil paints in tubes, all of them squeezed, disfigured, and seeping the same yellow sap from their cracks and creases.

A pile of canvases stacked up against the wall attracted his attention, with their faces turned away from sight. Next to them, three or four wooden frames, over which canvas material would one day be stretched, acted like custodians over the unseen pictures. Thomas tilted the works away from the wall and peaked at the first painting in the row. He saw a nude woman lying back on a white bed, the bowl of her pelvis tipped towards the viewer unambiguously.

The painter's easel stood centre-stage. It was a large wooden structure with adjustable batons and legs that splayed in a pyramid shape. Paint freckled the wooden legs and on the easel was the large canvas that Thomas recognised from the Potsdam trip. Next to the easel, a number of tools – a palette knife, a sponge, a paint mixer – lay on a small knee-high table so to be always at hand.

Jana followed him as he wandered through the space. She was calm. Her face was plump and fresh, attractive for being free of makeup. Her eyes were clear and sharp. Her mouth was equally clear-cut; her upper lip protruded over the lower lip in the way that a cake overhangs its baking tin. Thomas found her to be an appealing figure, for she carried an aura of thoughtfulness, patience and artistic freedom – qualities he couldn't help but admire.

'I hope you like the surroundings,' she said, casting a glance around the room. By way of an introduction to her studio, she explained how an artist who paints portraits must contend with two unruly elements. The first is a shifting source of light, since this leads to creeping shadows and faces that change their expression. It's for this reason that a well thought-out studio has its main window facing north. The second is a shifting sitter. For this affliction the foremost remedy is alcohol. She had adopted this trick after once lacing a dish of cat's milk with liquor in order that the animal might stay still long enough for her to paint it.

She then offered Thomas a glass of cherry schnapps, which he accepted, smiling at her gentle joke. She poured out two small glasses and handed one over to him. He was beginning to find the studio surroundings more than a touch convivial.

'Come, let's get you in position,' she said, as she brought over a chair for him to sit on.

With the artist's help, he adjusted his pose to match the one he had held in Potsdam. She directed him to a small shelf behind his shoulder on which he propped his elbow so that his hand dangled beneath. He remembered the roof terrace and how he'd put his arm onto the railings and linked the fingers of this hand with the fingers of the other. He could see the scene now, sat with the long table in front of him and Erich at the far end. In his imagination, the roof patio began to assemble all around him. Once he was ready, Jana retreated behind her canvas and began mixing her paints.

'What is this painting about?' Thomas asked after about ten minutes, as he relaxed into the stillness of his pose. He realised he was actually enjoying the sensation of being observed and painted.

'About?' Jana replied, only half-listening.

'Will it represent anything?'

Jana continued to dab away with her brush, finally saying, 'Why don't you tell me what you think it's about? I'd like to hear your ideas.'

'Well, I don't know. Maybe is it about… Berlin people? People like us?'

The artist didn't respond but went on painting.

'Perhaps it's about all of us,' he continued. 'Am I getting warm? We live in a city with a million different people, a million ideas, a million individual stories. It is a vibrant place but these are troubled times, don't you think? It is a place where many rivers meet. There are so many conflicting values.' He paused. 'Am I at all close? You know, I'm both interested and a bit of a novice about art.'

Jana looked up. 'Yes, I believe you are close.'

Thomas fell quiet and for the next hour held his pose whilst she worked on the painting. A deep, satisfied silence lay brooding over the room. After an hour, she asked if he was happy to continue. He agreed. Then after a further forty-five minutes, as she began to clean her brushes, squeezing them through a cloth rag and then dropping them into a jar of turpentine, he realised the session was finished.

He stood up and stretched. He asked, 'May I see the painting?'

She smiled sympathetically as she shook her head, as if to deny by kindness.

'Just a quick look,' he said. He was determined to see what lay on the other side of that great rectangle.

'You'll have to be patient,' she said. 'But I have to say, it's going very well.'

'Even more reason for me to see it. The masterpiece needs an audience!'

Finally the artist relented, gesturing for him to come round to her side of the canvas. Now he could see the full expanse of the work, the array of figures – characters frozen in paint, situated across the seven-foot stretch.

There was the terrace and the rooftop skyline behind. He saw his own figure first, which was mostly painted in except for a few square inches of raincoat. What seemed remarkable to him was the likeness that she had achieved, for he recognised himself entirely and without any misgivings.

On close-up inspection, he saw that the paint was somewhat sparing, that is, not infinitely detailed but loosely applied. He considered that not a single brushstroke could have been different to how it was, not without upsetting the accuracy and balance of the picture.

He saw himself now as part of the wider rooftop scene, looking across the long white tablecloth, past Ingrid towards Erich and Käthe at the other end of the patio. His dark hair was swept across like a tilted cap, his raincoat looked worn, world-weary and charismatic. On the left was Käthe, her hair short, the line of her back serpentine; on the right, Jana had painted her own image into the work: where she was stood pouring cider from a jug.

Thomas began to remember details of that day in Postdam. He recalled Käthe unpicking the creases and ruffles of the white cloth across the table. Others arranged the chairs whilst Erich was busy drinking and telling stories. The models held onto their poses until the painter's light came to an end, and then the wind came and the evening drew in.

Next to Käthe was Erich's figure, the scallywag drunk peering up at the sky in contented disregard. Circumstances had captured him wearing a pursed smile, a self-satisfied though not entirely self-conscious smirk. Such a glimmer allowed a chink of light into the work, and breathed humour into the image, though it was perhaps the most troubling aspect. For Erich's demeanour was at odds with the rest: he looked different, cut through with irreverence as he sat askew at the table with his leg outstretched and his body slung to one side. All this gave him a rather inscrutable air – he had been captured perfectly.

Just then, Thomas' focus on Erich suddenly brought a rising sense of confusion. As he peered more closely, he noticed Erich's eyes were painted with an inebriated redness, but more than that, he realised that there was the thin outline of a pair of glasses. Jana had painted him wearing spectacles. And not only that, they were a pair of round, wire-framed spectacles – just like Arno's.

Thomas knew Erich to have near-perfect eyesight. It was something that he prided himself on, being able to read the smallest print in the newspaper or a distant sign on the street. Besides which, in all the time he'd known him, Thomas had never seen Erich in spectacles.

'Why is Erich wearing glasses?' he wondered out loud.

'How do you mean?' Jana replied.

'Here.' He pointed at the canvas. 'Erich is wearing a pair of glasses. He doesn't wear them normally.'

'Yes, just a little touch that I thought worked.'

He didn't quite believe what he saw. 'Do you mean they were something you added yourself afterwards?'

'No, Erich had the glasses with him that day in Potsdam. As I remember, they were in his upper jacket pocket.'

'He had them in his pocket?'

'I suggested he put them on. Didn't you see him with them? He's lost them since, apparently, but I have my sketches from the day.'

'No, I didn't.'

'He was playing with them and put them on. I thought they gave him extra character.'

Thomas knew it was too much of a coincidence to ignore. It wasn't just a clue but also a sign that things just didn't stack up. He was alert to this new detail, as it provided another important step to unravelling the mystery that had dogged him so persistently.

'Those glasses must have belonged to Arno,' he said as he considered the possible chain of events. 'Erich must have encountered Arno before we even got to the roof terrace.'

'Arno?' Jana asked, returning to her brushes.

'That's Käthe's younger brother. The glasses don't belong to Erich, they belong to him. That explains why I found those glasses on the terrace.'

'Why does it matter?'

Thomas felt his resolve hardening. 'It matters because Erich told me he'd never met Arno before. Arno and Erich must already have been connected in some way, prior to that very evening.'

'Why don't you ask him?'

'I will. The next time I see him, I will ask him directly.'

'Today?'

'Today? Why do you say that?'

'Because he'll be here at any moment. He's coming for a sitting.' Jana looked up at the clock on the wall. 'Any moment now.'

Then, as if listening out for his cue, the studio door rattled with three heavy knocks and from behind it Erich's voice rang out true and unmistakable.

24

Erich entered the studio in the same manner that Thomas recognised so well: a bright, loose stride, a fierce grin on his face, the faint tang of expensive cologne, and a breezy sense that the world was watching him. Immediately, he took off his overcoat and hung it on a hat stand beside the hallway door. It was typical of Erich to make himself at home so quickly and to make a performance of it. When he eventually looked up, it took him a moment to notice the hardened face of his old friend across the other side of the studio.

'Thomas,' he hailed as he came forward. 'What a surprise! What are you doing here? I thought we were never going to see each other again?'

Thomas' first thought was to challenge him directly about the glasses in the painting. He knew instinctively that Erich had been lying about his acquaintance with Arno. The two of them had met prior to the night on the roof terrace, that was clear enough, but precisely how and why – and with what ramifications – Thomas was still yet to discover. Knowing he was close to the truth, he chose the more thoughtful option: he refrained from his initial impulse and instead greeted Erich with an amiable demeanour. The two friends shook hands and assessed one another.

'Have you come to see how I do it, pose I mean?'

176

Erich asked. 'Jana tells me I'm one of the best models she has ever known.'

The artist laughed with chagrin as she returned to her easel. Whatever was troubling Thomas about the painting, she decided it was best dealt with between the two of them.

'Are you okay?' Erich asked, sensing Thomas' poise. The last time they had met Thomas had been fired up and insistent; this time he was as tranquil as a lake.

'Never better,' Thomas replied. He was becoming more and more cool-headed, as if a winter chill was solidifying his emotions and sharpening his senses.

Erich turned to Jana. 'Did you know this man is my closest friend? It's been decades, hasn't it Thomas?'

'He's been modelling for me this afternoon,' Jana responded. 'We've made wonderful progress.'

'Well, that *is* good news. You have done a good turn today, Thomas.'

'If you say so,' Thomas said.

'Why don't you stay around for a while? I'd like to talk to you anyway. What do you say, old friend?'

'No, I must be leaving.'

'So soon? But you haven't even told me what you think of the painting.'

'I have an appointment to go to. As for the painting – it's revelatory.'

At this, Thomas began to make his retreat. He thanked Jana for her hospitality and bid Erich farewell. Then he made his way through the studio and closed the door behind him, just as Erich and Jana disappeared behind the canvas and out of view. Whilst appearing to leave he did not shut the door entirely. He waited on the landing for half-a-minute before silently creeping back into the studio hallway and making an immediate beeline for the hat stand. He took off his own hat and hooked it over the stand. He found Erich's overcoat, which hung from one of the pegs like the flayed skin of Saint Bartholomew himself.

Thomas was now possessed by an intense concentration that gave his movements the efficiency of a machine. His hands moved quickly, sifting through the folds of the coat, dipping methodically into each pocket in turn searching for something that would intimate what Erich was really up to. As he hunted through he kept glancing up to check on the others' whereabouts. The pockets of the overcoat where sprinkled with Erich's personal articles: a screwed up handkerchief, a handful of loose change, a half-spent packet of cigarettes – and with the cigarettes, another book of matches with the word *Beguine* written on.

Thomas knew there had to be more, there had to be something else here that would more firmly corroborate his nagging sense that Erich and Arno were connected. He put the matches back into the overcoat pocket and went on looking. And then, finally, he came across an object deep within one of the coat pockets: a large bronze key.

He pulled out the key and turned it over in his hand, feeling its weight in his palm. Tied around the end of the key was a paper tag with the word *Ruppin* written on it. He knew the word instantly: it was the name of the building where Käthe had her apartment. He'd seen the word on the carved stone cameo at the entrance. Was it a key to her apartment, and if so, what the hell was Erich doing with it?

Just then he heard footsteps behind him. He looked up and saw Erich strolling across the studio floor towards him.

'Everything okay,' Erich asked. 'I thought you had left us?' There was no alarm on his face, no sense that he was concerned with whatever Thomas might be up to.

'I just forgot my hat,' Thomas replied, plucking his hat from the stand. 'I'm forgetful like that.'

'Are you? I didn't know that about you.' Erich's eyes glanced towards his overcoat. Then he put his arm around Thomas' shoulder. 'Why don't we go out for a walk,' he said. 'Jana said she can wait for me.'

Thomas put up no resistance. They descended the stairwell in a deep silence that took him straight back to that morning in Potsdam. He remembered with perfect clarity how they went down the staircase at Käthe's apartment on their way to hunt for the missing body.

When they entered the street below the studio, Erich led Thomas to a dingy cobbled alleyway. 'It looks like I will have to leave Berlin for a while,' he said. His tone was uncommonly grave.

The admission took Thomas by surprise but he didn't show it. What was Erich up to?

'So,' Erich went on, 'you have one last chance to report me to the police.'

'It almost sounds as if you want me to,' Thomas replied. He pushed his hands into his pockets and felt the cool form of the bronze key with his fingers. If Erich suspected he had been through his coat, then he wasn't about to confront him about it.

'Well, are you going to report me?' Erich asked.

'How long do I have?'

Erich let out a long sigh. 'The trouble with Thomas is that you're just too loyal. We don't deserve you. None of us deserve you.'

Thomas listened. As he did, his eyes were caught by the sight of a figure passing along the end of the alleyway. The figure stopped briefly and looked directly at the two men. He was tall and wearing a bowler hat. He stood motionless for several seconds and then moved on.

'Are you in trouble?' Thomas asked Erich, sure that this was the same man he'd seen following him some days before.

'I can't say.'

'You can tell me.'

'I can't – if I do, it will put someone in danger.'

'Erich, what have you done?'

'We must be careful, we should have done this inside. I thought I knew you well Thomas, but I've underestimated you.'

Thomas could see his friend was deadly serious. 'We should leave,' Thomas said, knowing that it was time to part company.

They walked to the end of the alley, just as an electric tram rattled past. Erich glanced left and right, then up at a darkening sky. 'Rain,' he said, just as a large drop clashed onto his forehead. He let out a wretched laugh as he reached up to touch the wet spot with his finger.

'I'm leaving tomorrow,' he said.

'Where are you going?'

'I can't tell you, but believe me when I say I must disappear for a few weeks. It's safer if you don't know where. You must put me out of your mind for now, Thomas. Continue to make your own way. You will have your answers soon.'

Thomas made no response. He watched his friend go back into Jana's building and close the door behind him, then he turned and moved off in the opposite direction. The bronze key was still in his pocket. His next stop was Potsdam.

25

Thomas quickly mounted his motorbike and rode it out of the city towards Potsdam. He travelled through the darkening countryside where the lit windows of farmhouses reflected in the waterways and the trees swayed in hunched silhouettes. He arrived at dusk with the noise of iron-rimmed wheels turning over cobblestones. A horse and cart sat in the purple light and the three-pronged candelabra street-lamps were blinking into life. He rounded the corner of the main street, feeling the brilliant glow of the city on his shoulders. The air seemed suspended in this moment, as if dusk had paused and would last for hours.

He passed a small gathering of protesters carrying placards and singing *Freie Bahn dem Tüchtigen*. A boy with a tambourine banged a rhythm, keeping time with the melody. 'Make way for the brave,' Thomas repeated to himself as he went by. Outside Clärchens Bar, a soldier had accosted two women in fur coats and was handing them pamphlets. He was holding the wrist of one of them, smiling and snarling as he urged her to take a pamphlet.

At Käthe's apartment, Thomas took the stairs up to the hallway where a dim electric lamp hovered over the space with a cold-grey light. He forgot to knock and moved through the rooms swiftly, spaces he had come to know well, rooms that were marked in the deepest quarters of his memory. He called out her name.

'Thomas?' she called back from behind a wall. A moment later, Käthe appeared. She was wearing a knee-length evening dress, a glamorous shard of emerald-green that took her visitor quite by surprise.

'Have you come to see me? I haven't really got time right now, Thomas.' She seemed agitated. He noticed she was holding a bottle of wine in her hand.

'I need to see you,' he said.

'Need? It's been more than a week. Why would you need to see me all of a sudden? I thought you'd disappeared from Berlin.' She passed her hand through her short hair, a reflex she tried to subdue as soon as she was conscious of it. Her neck sparkled with a string of coloured stones, and on her ears, two pearl studs were clipped to the lobes. 'Well?' she asked insistently.

'I had other things to attend to.'

'You've come at a bad time – I'm in a terrible rush.'

She walked out of the hallway, leaving him in the company of the big rubber plant. Ahead of him he saw the passageway to the terrace.

'Käthe?' he said, following her through the apartment. 'Where are you going tonight?'

He found her checking herself in the bedroom mirror.

'Does it matter where? I'm seeing some friends from the office. Not that it's any of your business.'

'I've come to see you.'

'Where have you been Thomas?' Suddenly her cheeks blushed pink, warmed by her disgruntled manner.

'It hasn't been so long.'

'Eight days?' She posed the number as a question. 'And you didn't think to call or even make contact?'

He didn't answer. Suddenly the thought of waiting so

long to see her seemed ludicrous. He knew too well these familiar and hospitable surroundings, but the young woman stood before him took on a demeanour that was hard to read and distant.

'I've just been preoccupied with other things,' he stammered. Then he looked at her, sensing her disappointment. 'I can honestly say, that you've never left my thoughts in the last eight days Käthe.'

'What I don't understand' – she said, pausing now to find her composure – 'is that we were getting close, I even wanted you to meet my brother. Oh what's the use!' She laughed a strained, ironic laugh, and shook her head with her hand resting on the back of her neck.

'But it's because I've been looking for Arno that I have been absent!' Thomas exclaimed.

'Arno? Have you got news of him?'

'In a manner of speaking… Sort of.'

'Well I haven't got time right now to discuss this. I'm sorry Thomas. I have to go. I'll be late if I don't leave soon.' She began picking up her purse and lipstick from a side table and put them into her beaded handbag. She drew a hat over her head as she approached the front door.

'Wait,' he said blocking her path. He held up the bronze key that he had taken from Erich's coat. 'I need to ask you about this key, it's important.'

'Thomas! It will have to be another time.'

'It has to be now.' He handed the key over to her. 'I was hoping you would know what it's for.'

'Where did you get it from? It's looks like the key to my apartment.'

'That's what I thought.'

She immediately went to the cabinet on the wall of the hallway and opened its tiny wooden door to reveal the key-box. She unhooked a second key from the inside.

'No, it can't be my key,' she said shaking her head. 'I have mine here. It looks like my key, but it isn't.' She held up both the keys, side by side and indeed they looked identical to the naked eye.

'Could it be a copy?'

By way of checking, she took the key Thomas had given her and tried it in the front door lock. 'No, it doesn't fit,' she said swiftly, handing the key back to him. As she did, she pushed it soundly into his hand to reaffirm her impatience with the moment.

'Käthe, look, I don't know how but it may have something to do with your brother.'

She stopped. 'What's Arno got to do with it?'

'Have you seen him this week?'

'Arno? No I haven't.'

'When did you last hear from him?'

'I told you. It was about two months ago. I've placed an advert in the newspaper, look at this,' she said as she pulled out a copy of *Tempo* from the sideboard. Her finger pointed to a listing in the personal adverts column. Thomas read the words, '*Concerned relative seeks news on the whereabouts of Arno Hiller from Hallesches Tor, Berlin; last seen in April; nineteen years old, hazel eyes, wears glasses, occasional beard; urgent information thankfully received.*'

'Have you heard anything? Has anyone come forward?'

'No.' She looked at him in silence, then slipped the hat off from her head, a sign she would listen to what he had to say.

'We found his glasses, out on the terrace, didn't we? Remember?'

'Yes, of course.'

'And did you ask your aunt about them? Did she leave them here?'

'No, she didn't. She didn't know what I was talking

184

about.'

'So someone else must have left them.'

'Who?'

'It was Erich who left them. It was only today that I found out that he had the glasses with him on the day of the painting. I also found this key with the word *Ruppin* attached to it. I knew it couldn't be a coincidence, so I came over right away.'

'You're not making any sense. You're just worrying me. What else do you know about Arno?'

'I think we saw him, on the night we all came here for the painting. In fact, I'm positive we did.'

'Where?'

'In a bar. He came up to us, asking for help. I'm afraid he didn't look well.'

'Why are you only telling me this now?' Her voice became taut.

'I didn't know it was him! Not at the time anyway. But this key could explain something.'

She took the key from his hand and examined it again. 'It looks exactly like my apartment key but it's not. Perhaps it's for one of the other apartments.'

'How can we tell?'

'There's only one way to find out.' She slipped out of the front door and rushed down the stairwell. On the floor below, where four other apartment doors lined the narrow hallway, she went straight to the first door and put the key in the lock. It rattled but didn't turn.

'Not this one,' she whispered cautiously as Thomas followed down the stairs. He watched her move between the doors at a fearless pace. At the next door, she put the key in and tried to twist it but the lock didn't move.

At the third door, she put the key into the lock and this time her wrist began to turn. She looked back at Thomas. 'This is it,' she said as her eyes widened. She

185

turned the handle of the door and went inside.

26

Käthe moved ahead, creeping through, not knowing whether to feel relieved or frightened, or anything else for that matter.

'Let me go first,' Thomas said in a hushed voice, stepping ahead of her. It suddenly occurred to him that he had no idea what they would find inside. Had Erich somehow returned and moved Arno's body into this apartment? Would they find Arno's corpse slumped in an armchair, decomposing from a month of waiting to be found?

The scene that presented itself defied anything they might of expected. At first, no discernible furniture was apparent; instead, there was a chaos of white paper, some of it in piles, some of it bound into batches, most of it scattered across the floor in a kaleidoscope of white tiles that shifted with the breeze from the open door.

The smell was odd. A faded musty air deepened by something recognisable. Thomas found it familiar, in fact he knew it well from Berlin, from somewhere in the city. The answer was plucked easily from his memory – it was printing ink! It was the same coagulating smell that he breathed at the newspaper print rooms, the same heavy fog that filled his nostrils each night at the *Berliner*.

Käthe picked up a bundle of papers. 'What on earth are these?' Then she read aloud from one of them. '*No justice for vigilante hero.'*

Thomas reached for another batch. *'Defend our nation from Communist criminals,'* he read.

They looked at each other. 'What is this?' Käthe asked.

'It looks like they're being printed here,' Thomas replied, at the same moment noticing a small hand-operated press in the far corner of the room. 'They're pamphlets. But for what purpose?'

'To influence public opinion – propaganda,' she said. The prospect of its manufacture, there under her very nose, gave her a spike of trepidation.

Ahead of them, several rooms led off through open doorways. The hundreds of sheets of paper had momentarily distracted them from the possibility of danger ahead. Thomas' thoughts cycled between acute hesitation and the compulsion to understand Erich's motivation.

As it was, Käthe now led, stepping through the drifts and piles of paper towards the first room. Another pamphlet caught Thomas' eye. *Potsdam Hero Arrested For Murder.* He read the words silently to himself as he passed. *Hero of the nation arrested for throwing criminal boy from building. Communists conspire to destroy German freedoms. Liberate the nation's hero and protector!*

The words swayed and wobbled before his eyes. He could hardly comprehend what he was reading.

Hero of the nation arrested for throwing criminal boy from building, another stab in the back!

He let the paper drop to the floor. All at once, the poisons of civilised society seemed to converge on the hallway of that apartment. A stew of confusion passed through him like the ghoulish spirals of a bad dream. Now a window loomed up, and through it he could see the blue of the Potsdam night.

They turned a corner and went through a panelled door whose white paint was peeling badly. The apartment was in a terrible state. There was a large white sink into which water dripped from a rusty copper pipe. A steel cooking pan with scorch marks on its underside contained the remnants of scrambled eggs. Along the walls, a carved dado rail had furry mould growing on its lower edges. The smell of a coal-powered stove clung onto the walls. Overhead, a piece of string with wooden pegs was pinned across from one wall to another, used as an indoor washing line. On the far wall, a framed print showing Christ with His arms outstretched was faded from too much sunlight. More paper, some of it printed and some of it blank, lay in circles on the dirty floor. A open box of candles and a pile of books lay nearby.

Then, around the next corner, almost unbelievably, the face of a boy. The face of *the* boy. He was lying on a sofa with his feet resting on a woven-rush chair. There was a stack of clothes piled up over the backrest.

The boy looked up at the intruders. In his hands he was holding a battered Spanish guitar that, for now, he was paralysed from playing. The beard had been shaved off and his face was fresh, but it was certainly him. The vagrant in the tavern, the thief-boy on the roof terrace.

'Arno!' Käthe exclaimed.

The boy swung his feet onto the floor and stood up. His face was a dismal concoction of fear and amusement.

'My god! What are you doing down here?' she said, rushing over and embracing him. 'You're here, but what are you doing in this place?'

Thomas wouldn't speak. His sights remained fixed on the boy. A flush of relief swept through him as he let himself comprehend that the boy was – thank God – still alive.

189

Arno lowered his head to hide his awkwardness. He dug his hands into his pockets and tried to subdue a smirk from rising on his face. He began to justify himself to Käthe. He said he was just waiting for the right time to explain. Then, after a faltering start, he spoke more rapidly. He'd been living in the apartment for the last month. He said he was working for Erich, following Erich's orders. He said Erich had arranged and paid for everything. He held up a pile of hand-written letters – these, he said, came once or twice a week. They were instructions. Erich sent crates of food and boxes of candles and clean clothes, along with the letters.

Everything the boy said came interrupted with questions from Käthe, who simply couldn't understand why he would be living in the apartment beneath hers without telling her, especially in these conditions.

Thomas listened as he pieced it together, and then reached the point where he couldn't stay quiet any longer.

'How did you do it?'

'Do what?'

'How did you manage the deception out on the terrace? You made it seem as if Erich threw you over the railings? You made it appear that you'd fallen from the sheer height of the rooftop. How was it possible?'

Käthe looked at Thomas. 'What are you talking about?'

'Let him explain,' Thomas pointed at the boy, his voice rising in volume. 'Let your brother give us the truth.'

'It wasn't hard.' Arno replied coolly. 'We practiced it.' He went over to the living room window and with a rattle of the handle pushed it open. The window swung outwards. 'Up there,' he said pointing.

Thomas went over and together they stuck their

190

heads through the opening. Above, he could see several layers of brick and then the vertical black lines of the patio railings about ten feet higher. The apartment in which they were standing was directly beneath the roof terrace.

Arno went on, 'Erich had this old climbing equipment. I don't know where he got hold of it from. A metal hook, a rope, a harness. We practiced it, maybe twenty times, until we had it just right. He swung me over the railings and I came in through this window.'

'That's not possible,' Thomas said. 'I saw you go over. I saw you fall.'

'We fooled you,' Arno said, a prideful smile playing at the corners of his mouth.

'No, that can't be right. I heard you hit the ground. I swear it.'

Arno shook his head. He took the handle of the window and pulled it in firmly until it closed shut with a deep thud.

'I don't believe it,' Thomas said dumbfounded. 'That's what I heard, a window closing.'

'We rehearsed that too,' Arno said. 'I came in through the window, then waited, and then thump.'

Käthe, somewhat bewildered, said, 'I don't understand. Why would you do that?'

'To set the scene of a hoax,' Thomas answered. It was all becoming clear to him now, like snow melting in a city and the streets reappearing after the thaw.

'We practiced when you were out at work,' Arno said to his sister.

'But why?'

'Your brother and Erich staged it all in order to trick me,' Thomas answered, but before he could go on, more questions tumbled into his mind. He turned to Arno. 'But why all this? You're printing pamphlets – I can see

191

you want to provoke something – anger among people – for what purpose?'

Arno answered in a single sentence. 'We wanted the Communists to get the blame for Erich's arrest.'

'Erich's arrest?'

'That's right. For throwing me over.'

Thomas thought for a moment. 'That's where I came in. I was meant to lead Erich to the police.'

'Yes, but you didn't do it.'

'No, I didn't.'

'He thought that you were the ideal person. He said you were too honourable to resist. He said it might take you a week or maybe two, but your conscience would get the better of you in the end. So we've been waiting for you to play your part. After that, we would have put the next stage of the plan in motion.'

'You've been waiting all this time – for me to act?'

Arno nodded.

'But Erich's my friend,' Thomas said by way of an explanation. 'Besides, how could I go to the police when there was no trace of a body?'

Käthe came forward with another pamphlet in her hand. 'Some of these call Erich a hero.'

Thomas picked up a new batch of papers. Erich's name appeared all over them as if the very word was bubbling up across the paper.

'We intended to cast Erich as the vigilante,' Arno explained.

'So Erich gets arrested for taking the law into his own hands,' Thomas said. 'He gets called a hero. Then you stir up support for him under the pretence that the Communists are defending the poverty-stricken thief.'

'That's what we wanted,' Arno said. 'We wanted to create anxiety among true Germans by telling everyone that the Communists had sided with the criminal.

German politics is so polarised, we thought we could exploit that. We were going to campaign for Erich's release based on his patriotic deed, whilst also talking up the conspiracy against him. That's what I've been doing down here all this time. Printing these pamphlets. Then after a few weeks, once the interest had died down, I would turn up alive and he'd be set free.'

'But I didn't play into your hands.'

'Erich was wrong about you.'

'Do you know where he is now?' Thomas asked. 'He told me he has to leave Berlin. Disappear – why?'

'I don't know. All I know is that he's involved with some Brownshirts.'

'Nazis? Is that who you're doing this for?'

'He was concerned about what they might do to him if the plan didn't work out. You've got no idea what these people are capable of. They're all ex-military. He has to stay out of their way for a while.'

'So he failed. And now he has to go into hiding.'

Arno walked away from the window and crossed the room to a metal washbasin on a table, apparently unconcerned about Erich's fate. He splashed water on his face. 'How did you get in here?' he asked as he put a crumpled towel to his face.

'Using this.' Käthe held up the key.

Arno shrugged. 'So it's all over then,' he said. He dried his hands with the towel and seemed to relax, apparently enjoying relief at the end of the game. He sat down on the battered old sofa and said, 'I haven't heard from him in a week. At least I can leave this damned apartment now.'

'Why did you want to do this?' Käthe asked her brother. Her tone was insistent.

'This country is in disarray,' Arno replied. 'Ever since the war we've all been taken advantage of. I want to make our country strong again, and that begins with getting rid of the Communists, and the Jews for that matter.'

'What do you know about Communists and Jews?' Käthe said disparagingly. 'You're too young to know anything. Besides, they're people just like us.'

'I've lived! You don't know what I've seen. Just because you're my sister doesn't give you the right to lecture me. I know about the Bolsheviks. They only bring war and famine. We have to protect our land.'

As they argued, Thomas walked in circles around the room, remembering with vivid clarity the night in the tavern some weeks before, when he and Erich were approached by the young man asking about Orenstein and Koppel, the same young man who stood before him now. How incredible it all seemed. But Erich? Was he so against the Communist Party that he would risk his own imprisonment? And for what end? The scatter of paper around him gave clues: Erich and Arno intended to stir up resentment within the working classes and turn them against Communism. *Enemy Within! Subhuman Infiltration!* It seemed such madness, but then it was all here, all around his feet in these pamphlets, undeniable and alarming.

And then he remembered the story of the prostitute. That whole story of the woman that Erich said had been staying in his apartment… Gina. That story was surely a lie too. It seemed so obvious now, looking back. Erich had been laying a trap for Thomas all this time, getting him to feel sympathy for the downtrodden just like Gina. He thought back to what Erich had said on that day, about *looking after vulnerable people.* It was all a ploy to prepare him for the roof terrace, to give an impression of Erich that, in his subsequent ruthlessness, he would completely contradict by fatally punishing the thief-boy.

Was it meant to incite Thomas? To make him see Erich as a changed man, from sympathetic to deranged? A man whom he could more easily take to the police?

He turned back to face Arno. 'Did you ever have a fiancé?'

'What do you mean?'

'When you came to us in Clärchens bar, you said you had a fiancé.'

'No,' Arno replied.

'Children?'

'No.'

'Then you made it all up, so you would appear destitute and pitiful just to deceive me?'

Arno nodded.

Thomas put his hand in his pocket. He pulled out the wristwatch. 'And what about this?'

Arno took the watch and turned it over in his palm 'Oh yes, this.'

'What is it?' Käthe asked.

'Erich sent word ahead,' Arno said. 'He told me to do it.'

'Let me guess,' Thomas said. 'He told you to smash the watch and turn the time to six o'clock, then to leave it somewhere where I would find it.'

'That's right. Don't ask me how, but he knew you would come to Potsdam again looking for clues.'

'But I didn't find it,' Thomas said. 'A man gave it to me. A homeless man. He sold it to me.'

'Then he must have found it before you did. That was a stroke of luck, I suppose.'

Just then, Käthe called out, 'It's here.' In her hands she held the crystal decanter that she and Thomas had looked for several weeks before. 'To think that our aunt took it. It was you, Arno!'

Thomas came over, took the decanter from her and

placed it gently on the table.

'It's over now,' he said, as he glanced between the brother and sister. 'It's all over now.'

27

A month after the discovery that Arno had been living in the apartment below Käthe's, Thomas went to visit Ingrid. She handed him a letter. As he read it, she retreated to a doorway, holding her modestly swollen abdomen in two hands. Her long neck caught a ribbon of light whilst the rest of her lay in shadow.

A month or more of concern had now reached something of a climax, as she had received a note from Erich from a distant place giving broad clues to his whereabouts. He'd taken a train across France and then to Spain where he'd attempted to join a military academy in Zaragoza. 'People are awake here,' he wrote, 'because they know the plague is coming.' The fate of his parents seemed to concern him in particular: 'I'm sorry for them. I think of my Mother playing cards all day whilst Father stands and stares out of the window.' He spoke of 'pressures growing in America' and 'market troubles that could really destroy our great country if we don't protect it.'

Thomas passed his eyes over the writing, rendered in Erich's famous childlike hand. It seemed certain that circumstances were about to change. A new economic danger lurked in the realities of his family's estate. Erich, however, would not be around to see the ramifications. Any questions surrounding his responsibilities as a businessman, son or father, were answered with emphatic abnegation: 'I don't expect to be home for at least six months. When the baby is born, visit my parents and they will give you the help you need. Ingrid, please believe me when I say it: I'm sorry.'

Despite the illegibility of the ink, Thomas found the tone to be remarkably assured, poised intriguingly at the meeting place of adventurism and morose regret. 'First, I'm going to learn about the workers and the soldiers, by living with them and working alongside them. Second, I'm going to thwart the forces that make a political pawn of my brothers.'

In the weeks that came in its wake, Thomas felt not the least degree of surprise towards the letter. That Erich had abandoned his home and his family was consistent with his rejection of any sense of time and permanence. Despite all his high-mindedness, Erich's values had always been best expressed by impulsiveness. They were, by that very nature, ill-conceived – so Thomas judged them.

A veritable uproar followed the news from the letter amongst Erich's family members, who saw him only as a duty-bound individual. Disbelief and anger flared up in equal measure, succeeded later by the sort of disappointment that can only occur between blood relations. How he could abandon his duties, especially towards the mother of his baby, was impossible to fathom, and yet to his closest friends there was an eerie sense of acceptance. Ingrid exhibited both devastation and relief, and managed to find salvation in her infinite love for the unborn child. For Thomas, though he could barely admit it to himself, Erich's departure brought about a sense of deliverance.

The months of summer rolled on, and by August, a new

198

set of fortunes had come to shape Thomas' future. Herr Beenken collapsed one day at the top of the staircase and fell an entire flight whilst in a state of unconsciousness. His demise was sudden, swift and more or less painless. He never woke up; three days later he was dead.

Before that, Thomas had not seen Beenken for over a month. Their acquaintance had shifted from the regular visits to Thomas' room to the occasional swapping of glances in the hallway. The landlord's philosophy on life had adapted, and with it, his propensity to chit-chat: 'Take my word for it, don't trust anyone out there,' he'd said during their last conversation. 'It's not the same city anymore.'

'Why not?' Thomas responded.

'Foreigners, vagabonds, charlatans. They're all over the place.' He gestured to the building itself. 'They're even in here, swarming like rats.'

And then, a few days later, 'Thomas, I'm thinking of living alone for a while. Have you noticed that half of the rooms here are now empty? It's simpler that way. When they're vacated, I don't fill them again.'

Beenken had withdrawn almost entirely from life outside the building, and more or less from life inside it too. The only time he dared venture from his doorway was at eight o'clock in the evening when Thomas, duly stationed at the very bottom of the stairwell, was in place to pull a winch that carried a straw basket up two flights to Beenken's doorway. It was a system Beenken had designed himself and engineered at considerable cost, one that allowed him to receive mail and a small hamper of groceries without ever having to descend to street level or interact face-to-face with anyone.

Thomas performed his duty with neither satisfaction nor resentment. In fact, he didn't mind the obligation, since it coincided with him leaving for work every night.

Typically a piece of paper rode down with the basket. 'NEED MORE TOBACCO' it might read in large scrawl. Thomas wrote back 'TOMORROW' in the same sized letters and sent the basket back up. Without checking for a response, he left the building, thinking how sad the arrangement was, not least because it meant that Beenken was really a dying man.

Still, he had not imagined it would happen so rapidly, until the day he received a letter from Beenken's solicitor in his post box. He'd not seen the straw basket hanging by its cord for at least a week, maybe longer, and had assumed Beenken had procured someone else to do the winching. Then the letter came, and the absence of the basket was explained in more permanent terms. The solicitor gave no indication as to how it happened – Thomas learned the details of the fall later – but made a point of stating that the search for Beenken's next of kin had begun. Thomas' shock at the news quickly grew into curiosity. 'Why are they asking for me?' he said to himself as he prepared to leave for the offices of Beenken's solicitor for a meeting at the letter's request.

The answer supplied was simple and, at first, disquieting. Inconceivably, Beenken had named Thomas as the sole inheritor of his entire estate.

'I'm not taking on his debts,' was Thomas' first response.

'Oh, it's not like that,' the gentleman in the suit replied. 'It's not that way at all.'

'No?'

'No. Herr Beenken has no debts to his name; on the contrary, he owns, without a mortgage, the entire set of apartments in which you live.'

Thomas was stunned. He listened as the details were spelled out to him, how the estate consisted of all eleven rooms across three floors, as well as a set of garages, a four-hundred-square-foot cellar space and even the patch of land at the back of the building where Beenken once spoke of tethering a cow. To his astonishment, Thomas discovered that Beenken was an extremely wealthy man – with no next of kin.

'That can't be true. I thought he was just the landlord acting on someone else's behalf.' Thomas sat back in the solicitors' armchair, whose leather creaked as he shifted his weight. A strange combination of dismay and astonishment swept through him. 'I had no idea he owned it all.'

'He doesn't own it anymore. You do.'

'What am I going to do with it? I mean, I don't really have time to run all those rooms.'

'My advice would be to sell. Sell quickly! A plot of land at the end of the Kurfürstendamm would bring you more than a tidy sum.'

'The place is a wreck.'

'Let someone else worry about that,' the solicitor said as he leaned back in his seat. 'Believe me, you will find a buyer easily who will be willing to invest.'

'I don't believe it. Why me?'

'Was there anybody else that Herr Beenken was friendly with?'

'Not that I know of.'

'Then you have your answer.'

Thomas was struck with disbelief. Afterwards, he took a long walk around the neighbouring streets, hardly able to digest the news. Without meaning to, his mind slipped into daydreams of lavish living, of buying clothes and jewellery for Käthe and a new motorcar for himself. At the same time, he knew that living the life of luxury would take some getting used to!

To discover that someone as pitiful and needy as old Beenken could be in possession of such wealth was difficult to understand. It simply made no sense! Except perhaps to imagine that the building, with its rooms and tenants, was Beenken's way of being among people. He could have sold the place and become rich. Instead, he chose to keep it and have the company of his residents. Thomas began to realise that this was the choice Beenken had made; and began to understand the role he must have played in the life of the old landlord.

28

Jana Constein's finished painting had been kept in storage for several months whilst a gallery space could be found. It was now to be put on display at the respected Mattias Lassner Gallery on the Mulackstrasse. There would be four of her works hanging in the exhibition, including *The Roof Terrace at Potsdam*, along with paintings by other graduates from the Berlin Academy.

A number of small handwritten invitations were sent out to a list of significant collectors, and two weeks before the official opening one such invitation was pushed beneath Thomas' door, a piece of folded card which read '*Exhibition Preview Evening for Specially Invited Guests. 16th September 1928. Doors open at 6:30pm.*'

On the afternoon of the exhibition, two hours before it was due to begin, Thomas was already spruced up in one of his father's suits. He had an fresh flower in his buttonhole and his shoes were buffed to a glossy shine.

Should he take a drink from the brandy bottle? Yes, it was a special occasion. He had a small glass, ate a snack of bread, butter and ham, read a newspaper, had another quick brandy, and then walked out into the big night toward the gallery on the other side of town. He had not ridden his motorbike in weeks.

He arrived at the gallery fifteen minutes after the doors opened. The main room was already filled with people looking at the paintings on the walls, stood in groups chatting and exchanging opinions. By appearance, they seemed to be a well-heeled set of art lovers, many of them up-and-coming youngsters with confidence in their bones and a charming, easy-going style. Thomas followed protocol and began to move around the room peering closely at the pictures one at a time.

He examined the first couple of paintings he came to, raising his eyebrows as if the works surprised him, pursing his lips to suggest insight, and then moved on to the next section of wall. After only a short spell, he grew restless with this and began scouring the room for familiar faces. Within moments his searchlight had picked out his fellow models scattered here and there. Käthe and Ingrid were near to each other making up part of a small coterie, none of whom he recognised. Close by was the artist herself, greeting all the guests as they came through the doorway. Thomas went over to Jana and tapped her on her shoulder. He had not seen her since his last sitting.

'Thank you for coming Thomas,' she said, rather relieved and a little nervously. She was dressed very smartly, wearing a fine looking trouser suit in tribute to the importance of the event.

'I'm glad to be here,' he replied. 'There's such a lively atmosphere. Congratulations. How do you feel?'

'A mixture of elation and with a pinch of suspense. It's a heady concoction.'

'Is our painting here?'

'Of course, in the next room. Everyone I've spoken to seems to like it.'

'Well, that's great.' Thomas turned to glance towards the next room. He was about to comment on one of the other paintings, but by the time he turned back, Jana had

204

already been accosted by another guest. He decided to move into the next room and find the roof terrace painting. As he went, he wondered if he might be recognised by his portrait. Was he already famous for having his face immortalised in paint? But really, nobody seemed to be taking much notice of him.

The next room was just as lively as the first. Listening out, he could hear jokes being made, followed by the compliment of laughter soon after. He moved through, admiring the artworks as he went, not committing to any piece for too long but sipping on the atmosphere, glancing this way and that and looking to see if there was anyone he recognised. Everyone seemed happy, and for the first time in months he wished to hear Erich's voice talking to him. His old friend would have been in his element at the gallery, full of stories and enthusiasm. Rumour had it that he was coming back to Berlin, but nobody could say exactly when.

Before he reached Jana's painting, Thomas was grabbed by the shoulder. 'What a success!' a voice called out. It belonged to a startling looking woman, her eyes vivid and wide, and cheeks drenched in carmine. Later, Thomas would discover her to be Frau Lassner, wife to the gallery owner. 'This is the real thing – great Berlin art! Are you interested in buying something today, sir?'

'A painting – I hadn't considered it. Are they collectors' items?'

'That depends. These works' – she gestured with both hands as if to pray to the walls – 'these are at the very cutting edge. Jana Constein's renown is growing by the day. I've already had expressions of interest in several pieces.'

Thomas smiled, thinking that he might mention his part in the roof terrace painting. Then, on the other side of the chattering crowds, he saw Ingrid approaching. She walked with a huge mound on her front and her legs planted apart to steady herself. Despite her excess size, to Thomas she seemed smaller than usual. He went over to her and bid his greeting, then asked how she was feeling, attempting to load his question with allusions to her wider health. She responded with little more than a sigh. 'I'm feeling tired actually. Thank you for asking. I'm ready for my baby, ready to be a mother,' she said, raising a sober smile.

'Perhaps we can find a chair for you.'

'I would like that.'

He went off to find something suitable. On his return, he was greeted by an elderly man who wore a scarlet polka-dot scarf around his neck. As the next few moments of ebullient conversation would reveal, this was Mattias Lassner, the owner of the gallery himself.

'Just one moment,' Thomas said to the old man as he took a stool over to Ingrid. He whispered to her as she sat down, 'I may be about to do something reckless.'

He returned to Herr Lassner. 'There is no doubt we are in the company of masterpieces today,' Thomas said with overdone certainty.

Herr Lassner agreed. Though he was of mature years, he had a strong and colourful voice. Closer inspection revealed that he too was wearing rouge on his cheeks, and that a slight lisp in his speech was caused by an ill-fitting set of false teeth. 'When shows like this come along, I'm so happy, because' – he raised his hand and pushed his teeth back into place – 'even the frames become priceless. Historians will talk about this moment for decades. We will all be placed under their scrutiny, believe me.'

Thomas smiled.

'And do you know,' Herr Lassner went on, 'I am touched by the personal impact of these works. To look upon such beauty and expression, that is no small mercy.'

'No small mercy indeed,' Thomas replied.

'Will you be purchasing tonight?' the old gent asked carefully.

'I'm giving it some thought. The large painting, in the other room, by Fräulein Constein, is a piece I'm particularly interested to see.'

'That's wonderful, let's see it together.'

'I'd be delighted to, but – '

'Please follow me.'

'I should stay here.' Thomas paused and glanced over to Ingrid.

'Go with him,' she said. 'I'm fine here.'

Thomas followed the gallery owner, weaving through the assembled guests until they were standing in front of the painting.

'*Roof Terrace at Potsdam,*' Herr Lassner announced.

'It's very fine,' Thomas said as he looked up at the work. It was so vivid. The way the light fell across the terrace and the figures were painted in such detail, it could almost be a real scene right before his very eyes. It was marvellous, with the whole painting finished and every brush stroke in place, glowing now under the adroitly positioned lamp shining down on it.

'How much does it cost?'

Herr Lassner made a play of consulting his notebook, as if the price was a mere triviality he would not deign to actually remember.

'Six thousand marks,' he eventually said in a hushed tone.

'That's a handsome sum!' Thomas said.

'Sir, this is the prize item of the exhibition.'

'Indeed, I'll take it.'

Just at that moment, he felt someone arrive by his

side. It was Käthe. She gave him a private nod and a delicate smile. He felt her fingers locate his, and side by side, they silently interlaced their hands as they turned their minds towards that familiar rooftop view together, upon which a new era had begun.

29

As autumn approached, the shades of the Tiergarten ebbed towards red, ochre and gold. At the weekends, Thomas left Berlin and spent the nights in Potsdam. In the mornings, he ate breakfast with Käthe in the small kitchen, then wandered out onto the terrace whilst she dressed, and taking a seat to the left side where the view over the city was best, he drifted into a listless state, peering over the tangle of rooftops as the sun dazzled upon his eyelids. He closed his eyes and allowed the orange-red patterns of light to mingle almost sensuously with the memories of the last few days.

How life had shifted. It had taken just four weeks to sell the apartment building in Berlin as a single going concern. In the event, the initial asking price was easily exceeded thanks to a clamour of interested speculators; in the bidding war that followed, another thirty-thousand marks was added onto the final selling price.

On the day after the sale, he was greeted by Malik at the front door who was holding a large paper bag filled with oranges. He set the bag down on the step and proposed the fruit to be a gift for his ex-roommate.

'It's been wonderful!' he shouted, 'but all things must end. These are for you, Thomas, as a thank you.'

'Where will you go?' Thomas said, feeling sentimental over the young student.

'I've taken a place on the south-side, half the rent – so don't worry about me. I'll be well looked after by new friends. Now please, have an orange.'

Malik picked up the bag and pushed it towards Thomas, causing several of the fruits to dislodge and roll into the road. Thomas grabbed one before it disappeared beneath the wheels of a cart and began to peel it open. He thanked Malik and asked who his new friends were.

'Some affiliates of, well, friends of friends, let's say. We have formed an important movement.' He waved his hand in the air ceremoniously. 'You will see us on the streets soon!' he said, adding, 'And you? Where are you going Thomas?'

'I've taken an apartment not far from here, just temporarily. The rooms are bigger than here. Where I go after that, only time knows the answer.'

'It's no coincidence that fortune has favoured you,' Malik said, adopting his wise-man tone. He was about to say more, to lavish compliments in the way he enjoyed to do, but Thomas interrupted to save his embarrassment.

'Are you sure you've got everything?' he said, watching as Malik struggled to gather up his belongings: beneath his arm he had a collection of books, and in each hand a suitcase. Between his fingers he clasped a copy of the *Lokalanzeiger*, a newspaper of satirical cartoons and scandal.

'I might have left a few things. They can be gifts to whoever takes the room.' Then, as he waddled off down the street he called, 'You and old Beenken were the best friends a man could have.'

'Silly young Malik,' Thomas whispered to himself as he waved goodbye.

The ten o'clock church bells chimed and woke Thomas from his reverie. By midday, he and Käthe were strolling beneath the ash trees of the Sanssouci park. Walking and chatting, he conveyed his fond memories of his household friends. 'I don't mind admitting, I'll miss them both.'

They sat on the grass. 'I just wish we could have given Beenken a more lavish finale,' he said as he thought of the marginal plot in the state cemetery. Beenken was given a basic funeral service, watched over only by Käthe, Malik and Thomas.

'You did your best,' she said. 'Let's face it, he didn't have many friends. Underneath, he probably would have preferred a quiet send off.'

Later, as they walked through the park, they came upon a concert hall where a performance was taking place that same evening. It was busy outside the venue. Queues of people bustled to snap up the last remaining seated tickets; the rest would have to make do with whatever standing room was left. Käthe opted immediately for a standing ticket and wasted no time in pushing past the shoulders and handbags of the people who still couldn't decide. 'I know the very best place to stand,' she said.

When it was time for the concert to start, she took them to a certain spot in the hall where, so she explained, the acoustics were at their best. There also happened to be a small step onto which she climbed to see above everyone else's head. When the orchestra emerged from behind a curtain, the audience began to clap, and Käthe made more noise than anyone.

The musicians were dressed in glistening black suits and immaculate haircuts. They took up their instruments in unison whilst a photographer came forward with his tripod. Much fuss was taken over the preparation of the flashbulb; the musicians stood quiet and still, occasionally adjusting their bow ties and well-trimmed

211

moustaches. Finally the flashbulb flared, and the crowd in the front few rows began a round of applause.

Meanwhile, the orchestral noises had begun, the period of tuning and limbering up, a whistle of a flute here, a drone of an oboe there, a practice drum-roll, a clarinet, a cello, all slowly but steadily converging on the single tuning note, louder and louder until it eventually overwhelmed the hum and murmur of the waiting audience, at which point everyone fell quiet. The performance was about to begin.

Now the conductor took to the stage, welcomed by another round of applause. He thanked the audience with his silent bow, then turning, raised his arms and incited the musicians to bring their instruments to the ready. Käthe looked at Thomas with a grin and he widened his eyes in agreement. The conductor's baton swooped, then with a pluck of a bass note from the string section, the music started up: rousing, loud and turbulent. The music thundered through the room, beckoning the audience to enter into the performance.

After the concert, the pair found a coffeehouse to relax in. Käthe's face was lit up with animation, a kind of impermanence that told of genuine happiness. Soon, she said, they would set up home in Berlin. For now, her Potsdam apartment was a fine nest for their fledgling love affair.

Over the following few months they spent every weekend together in Potsdam. Beneath an autumn sun that seemed focused into a rare and vivid beam, like a spotlight that followed the pair wherever they went, their romance bloomed. Thomas would later recall how their lips seemed constantly fused and their fingers always awake. The tips of all ten of his fingers fidgeted insatiably, as they wound around her hair and down her neck. The gloss of her skin was like an ice-rink for his

212

skating fingertips, where pirouettes spiralled upon apricot-white skin that glowed like snow-piles, or better still, sand-dunes, soft and firm at the same time, made up of a million crystals, in each an entire universe.

Käthe preferred to wash in the evenings. Sometimes Thomas found himself loitering at the door to the bathroom, just listening to the sound of water being scooped up and allowed to fall. He sometimes sat with her while she washed, crouched on her bare feet, kneeling, the long curve of her back defined against an oak chest of drawers behind, her skin white and shiny like the bark of a silver birch tree. He watched as she took the yellow sponge laden with water and swept it across her body, cascading liquid that dribbled and dripped onto the floor.

Now the very last stream of sunlight squeezed through the long window behind her and lit everything to a glisten. He took a long contented breath, as he went to the terrace for the final moments of sundown. A straw-coloured beam of light seeped across the patio and cast an indefinite pattern of colours on the floor. He put his hands on the railings and looked out. From here he could sense the town's history, and could almost touch its luscious baroque buildings and its hundred-year old trees, its parks and concert halls where old orchestras played. Then, as the skies turned purple, there was nothing left but the cold terrace, set in shadow as the town shut her eyes.

His mind returned to Berlin, the city that would glow like an ember all through the night. He felt a pulse of electricity move through his body: the energies of optimism and choice, both steadfast and bold. These strengths, which he realised had been rising in him over months, now lay brooding on his consciousness like the gauzy bloom of light that hung above the great city at night, marking the presence of the metropolis in the starry sky. And as he felt these energies move through him, he wondered, 'What did life have in store for him next?'

AUTHOR'S NOTE

Anyone who writes about the past has to contend with the gulf of historical distance, a space into which errors and anachronisms can easily fall. So whilst every effort has been made to accurately capture the historical details of Berlin and its environs during the Weimar years, it is worth noting that the characters in this book are not based on real people, either living or dead – with the exception of the artist Lotte Laserstein.

Her 1928 painting, *Roof Terrace at Potsdam*, was the original and abiding inspiration for this novel; it felt imperative, therefore, that she appeared as a figure in the story. I have, however, changed her name within the novel to Jana Constein, since the story she is embedded in is entirely fictitious and bears little relation to her actual life.

As a fond admirer of Lotte Laserstein's artwork, it is important to make clear that any errors or fanciful details are entirely my responsibility and should not influence the reputation of her own personality or art.

FIND OUT MORE

Thank you so much for reading Thomas' story. I hope you enjoyed your time with him in Berlin 1928. If so, it would be great if you could leave a review on your vendor of choice.

Would you like to read more? I have a free epilogue to *Berlin Vertigo* available to read.

Find out what happened next in Thomas' story:

Download the epilogue for free at:
https://BookHip.com/WQMBJF

Thank you.

Christopher P Jones

To find out more, go to www.chrisjoneswrites.co.uk

NEXT STORY IN THE BERLIN TALES SERIES

Vanished in Berlin
The follow-up novel to *Berlin Vertigo*

The story continues in 1931...
When Monika Goldstein, a young Jewish woman goes missing, Arno Hiller begins a desperate search to find her. But his hunt must come at a dark price.
As events speed up, Arno is forced to collaborate with the unpredictable Nazi Party. Set in the grip of corrupt officials and dangerous politics, he must choose his moves carefully.
Will his enemies trust him?
Or has he already lost Monika forever?
Both Monika and Arno take fate into their own hands, as they fight against the powers that are taking Berlin into fascism.
Told from the intimate perspective of two lovers caught between love and danger, *Vanished in Berlin* is an immersive and evocative suspense set in the seething world of 1930s Germany.

Vanished in Berlin is out now.